THE LEGACY SERIES

Series Titles

The Effects of Urban Renewal on Mid-Century America and Other Crime Stories
Jeff Esterholm

What Makes You Think You're Supposed to Feel Better
Jody Hobbs Hesler

Fugitive Daydreams
Leah McCormack

Hoist House: A Novella & Stories
Jenny Robertson

Finding the Bones: Stories & A Novella
Nikki Kallio

Self-Defense
Corey Mertes

Where Are Your People From?
James B. De Monte

Sometimes Creek
Steve Fox

The Plagues
Joe Baumann

The Clayfields
Elise Gregory

Kind of Blue
Christopher Chambers

Evangelina Everyday
Dawn Burns

Township
Jamie Lyn Smith

Responsible Adults
Patricia Ann McNair

Great Escapes from Detroit
Joseph O'Malley

Nothing to Lose
Kim Suhr

The Appointed Hour
Susanne Davis

Praise for
Jeff Esterholm

"Jeff Esterholm's excellent *The Effects of Urban Renewal on Mid-Century America and Other Crime Stories* feels like Raymond Carver by way of the Coen Brothers. These stories burn with deep place knowledge, and they're succinct, sharp, brimming with desperation and desire and dark humor. Esterholm writes characters who burrow under your skin. One of the best collections of short crime fiction I've read in recent memory."

—William Boyle
author of *Shoot the Moonlight Out* and *City of Margins*

"I've been writing about northwestern Wisconsin, particularly Superior, for fifty years. Now Jeff Esterholm comes along to show me what I didn't know. If you want to learn about this area and our fair city, about the tough men and women living up here, about the crimes real and imagined, the bleak winters and springs, Esterholm is the perfect escort. His characters look for trouble. The city itself is troubled. Maybe the neon of a North End tavern or the lake boats calling in the lonely night brings out the worst in people. One thing I know is Esterholm can write."

—Anthony Bukoski
author of *The Blondes of Wisconsin*

"*The Effects of Urban Renewal on Mid-Century America* by Jeff Esterholm is noir fiction to read and reread to savor all the nuances of the people and place of the story. It is a story set in a time but can be 'felt' in any time. It is peopled with folks who live dark lives without knowing exactly the why's or how's of how it all happened. One line that sticks with me is 'Joanne...fluffed the bouffant that was no longer there.' That line tells history, story, despair, hope, all in such sparse wording. A compelling read."

—Marcie Rendon
author of *Murder on the Red River*, *Girl Gone Missing*, and *Sinister Graves*

"*The Effects of Urban Renewal on Mid-Century America* offers something truly special: it's not only a consistently entertaining read, but also gives readers a harrowing—if often deadly—glimpse into the American psyche. Jeff Esterholm deftly reveals the essence of his characters with every line, as they're caught between an ever-present rust belt malaise and a deep yearning for something more. While the stories are set in mid-century America, they also contain a certain timelessness, as if representing a piece of the country that has always existed and may well continue in lonely pockets like the fictional Port Nicollet. This is a master storyteller at work."

—C.W. Blackwell
author of *Hard Mountain Clay*

"Jeff Esterholm's collection is the Great Lakes Noir you've been waiting for. On the icy edge of Lake Superior, the residents of Port Nicollet chase their dreams of wealth, escape, revenge, sex, and love—and bring tragedy upon themselves and others. Glowing with period detail, deep empathy, and wry humor, Esterholm's brisk tales take unexpected turns that always feel exactly right. Despite the danger, you'll want to remain in Port Nicollet long after the stories end."

—Ann Gelder
author of *Bigfoot and the Baby*

"Wielding the powers of an historian, linguist, and raconteur, Esterholm's crime stories capture the passage of nearly a hundred years in murder and deceit along America's longest coast—the forgotten 'Third Coast' of the Great Lakes, abattoir of stillborn cities and dreams, where last winter's secrets melt fresh from the snowbanks each spring. Imaginative and penetrating, these often brutal, occasionally humorous stories are crime fiction at its best."

—Zakariah Johnson
author of *Mink: Skinning Time in Wisconsin*

"These stories whir and hum, many with such a forceful echo of a bygone era it's as if they're delivered through the crackle of a Philco radio. Jeff Esterholm's elegant prose will draw you in and keep you comfortable right up until the well-timed reveals render you speechless."

—Curtis Ippolito
author of *Burying the Newspaper Man*

"Esterholm's stories are full of splendid grit, but they also ache with humanity. His characters are deeply realized and will break your heart . . . in a good way."

—Nick Kolakowski
author of *Love & Bullets* and *Boise Longpig Hunting Club*

"In these heartbreaking tales of the profane and the passionate, comedic, and doomed, Jeff Esterholm captures the historic and contemporary ghosts haunting the Upper Midwest in this striking collection. Esterholm's beer-drinking soul fills the pages with compassion as his characters navigate a world full of endless troubles."

—Tim Hennessy
editor of the *Milwaukee Noir* anthology

"Jeff Esterholm's compact prose offers us his South Shore world of loneliness and longing, of dread and despair, love and loss, of characters on edge who haunt a place-time just beneath the letter of the law, seemingly within arm's length of rock-bottom. You'll want to linger in Port Nicollet, and savor these clean and powerful stories."

—Steve Fox
author of *Sometimes Creek*

THE EFFECTS OF URBAN RENEWAL ON MID-CENTURY AMERICA

AND OTHER
CRIME STORIES

JEFF ESTERHOLM

Cornerstone Press
Stevens Point, Wisconsin

Cornerstone Press, Stevens Point, Wisconsin 54481
Copyright © 2023 Jeff Esterholm
www.uwsp.edu/cornerstone

Printed in the United States of America by
Point Print and Design Studio, Stevens Point, Wisconsin

Library of Congress Control Number: 2023937893
ISBN: 978-1-960329-08-0

Cornerstone Press titles are produced in courses and internships offered by the
Department of English at the University of Wisconsin–Stevens Point.

DIRECTOR & PUBLISHER   EXECUTIVE EDITOR
Dr. Ross K. Tangedal   Jeff Snowbarger

SENIOR EDITORS
Lexie Neeley, Monica Swinick, Kala Buttke

PRESS STAFF
Carolyn Czerwinski, Grace Dahl, Zoie Dinehart, Kirsten Faulkner, Brett Hill, Kenzie
Kierstyn, Maddy Mauthe, Natalie Reiter, Maria Scherer, Cat Scheinost, Anthony
Thiel, Chloe Verhelst

For Suzette

STORIES

Frenesí

*Port Nicollet, Wisconsin,
on the south shore of Lake Superior, 1941*

The Philco radio on top of the chest of drawers, prominently placed among the framed family photographs and two tortoiseshell vanity sets, dial glowing, played big band music broadcast from a station in Duluth. Artie Shaw's "Frenesí." The two sisters, Honor, the older of the two at twenty-four, and Faith, shared the double bed in the flat above their father's old shop. Faith was quiet that night, and when she spoke, matter-of-fact, Honor might have expected tears. A young man, passing through. Honor cradled Faith.

"I'll take care of it tomorrow."

Faith rolled onto her side, up on an elbow, and looked at Honor in the dim light. "How?"

"I will. Don't you worry. Tomorrow night. And afterward—yes, afterward—we'll drive over to Abigail's."

Faith blinked, her luminous eyes tapping out a code.

"I'll take care of it all, Faithie."

* * *

They used the shop's '39 Ford panel truck the first night they left a delivery at the hog farm. "It's gravy," Honor said to her sister. They drove back the three dark blocks to the flat and pulled in behind the building. One looked at the other, both

1

with pursed lips. And then they blew up, laughing. Giddy. They had gotten away with it, and paid to boot.

* * *

Abigail slipped from her robe—Rubenesque, Nels thought, a creamy blue nighttime dream—pulled back the covers and climbed back into her bed.

He was ready. She threw her leg over his hip. "What was that all about?" he asked, that business outside her front door.

"Your sisters." She chuckled. "Asking if you'd be coming home tonight."

"My sisters?" He sat up, or tried to.

Abigail's full-throated laugh was operatic. A contralto, she had left town twenty years before to sing opera, first in Minneapolis, then Chicago, and, almost, in New York City. For her own reasons, no one in town knew the why of it, but there were stories, she came back to her hometown. Now she raised Duroc hogs in Port Nicollet. "I told those girls, 'Not until after he comes here tonight.'" She pulled him back down among the wrinkled and gray pillows and sheets.

* * *

Edward—Nels, Faith, and Honor's father—was *the* butcher in Port Nicollet's North End. Quality beef, pork, chicken, and duck—the duck fresh on order, taken in the marshland along the lake—always available at Lund Family Meats. Edward Lund was also a well-known drunkard and that rotgut whiskey he loved so well killed him after a fashion. The widower was sixty-three years of age, riding home one late night on the historic last trip of the Beacon Avenue streetcar line—the transit authority scheduled bus service to begin the next day—when, expecting his stop, he prematurely exited the car. Edward swung out in a forward roll that tumbled him in front of the car that continued on its final trip down the tracks, grievously slicing him beneath its iron wheels.

Lund Family Meats ended up in Honor's strong hands in 1940.

Of Edward's children, Honor was the only one who took an interest in the trade. She was the one who applied herself, learning the skills Edward prided himself on. The other two, they were more interested in building box-karts and hurtling down the incline of the packed dirt alley that cut their block in half, or diving from the pilings of a disused pier into the cold, gunmetal swells of Lake Superior. No. Neither of the other two took an interest in the family butcher business like Honor.

Early on, she had taken to the shop hacksaw, feeling comfort, gaining knowledge in the impression made by her father's hand, worn as it was into the wooden grip, and the saw's smooth, near-silent rasping cut. The hacksaw, yes, second only to the meat cleaver. She had imagined the cleaver's quiet slicing flight through the air, accompanied by the guttural grunt that her father always made, before the jarring, wet hewing through meat and bone. The cleaver had passed from her grandfather to her father to Honor, the grip landing with its heft in her hand. The blade was a work of art: on one side, the etching of a beef cow, and on the other, a hog, both fine line depictions of these pastoral farm beasts before slaughter.

The business was now Honor's, and business was good.

* * *

Weekends, Honor and Faith stepped out, hoofed it to the jive of big band swing at the downtown clubs—Pearl's, the Shanghai, the Top Hat—strung out below the white lights of Beacon Avenue and Third Street. None of the clubs were like the nightclub in that MacMurray-Stanwyck picture, *Remember the Night*, that the sisters saw at the Palace last winter, where prosecutor Fred takes starved klepto Barbara for dinner and a turn on the dance floor. Booths, tables, the shining dance floor, the bandstand. All Honor and Faith had to do was squint, dim and blur the scene, and the skewed vision was enough to transport them into a club of high society in New York City or Hollywood, California, away, if for only a few hours, from Port Nicollet's provincial twenty-odd thousand, where the rural bled yet into the urban.

The night Honor was not with her, Faith, better known to the weekend jive bombers as Miss Hollywood, was on the beam and dancing on the city's nightclub circuit with their kid brother, Nels. They chugged into Pearl's on Third while the Cal Sundman Band, featuring Sandra Zwicki, late of Butternut, on occasional vocals, chuff-chuff-chuffed, woo-wooed! with "Tuxedo Junction," the engine woofing, locomoting down the rails, driving iron wheels always forward. Miss Hollywood—like a starlet hanging on the telephone for Mr. DeMille, hair, makeup, dress, say, yes, dressed to kill—took to the floor with très sharp Nels, meant to choogle on through the night, station, as it were, to station.

Nels, after a few dances with his sister, begged off, wanted to bug out. He was set for a stint in the U.S. Army and wanted to make the most of his remaining days and nights in Port Nicollet. Though he enjoyed himself, cutting the rug with Miss Hollywood wasn't all that he had in mind.

"Hey. Sis?" He mugged. He moaned.

"Abigail awaits?" She sipped her rum fizz, eyeing Nels over the rim of the glass. The local opera singer in retirement had popped little brother's cherry. It was common knowledge in the neighborhood. Also well-known, from the postman to the milkman, was that he couldn't help returning to the well on a nightly basis. Faith shook her head. What could she do with Mr. Woodpecker? He looked too young for the service. And no matter where he ended up, how could he stand being away from his sugar?

Nels clowned, fluttered lustlorn lids, and said, "You a fortune-teller or what, Miss Hollywood? Of course. I want to run over to Ab's and give her the scoop about me and Uncle Sam's contract."

She tried to muss his slick, full-on pompadour, but he ducked. "You're good. Get out of here."

"Jeez, thanks, Faithie." Nels kissed her cheek and was gone.

*　*　*

It began with the pie-faced boy from Cleveland who approached her after Nels, that horny pup, ran out. The boy—twenty-two, he said, in port on a boat taking on wheat from the Dakotas—she recognized as a dead hoofer, couldn't dance a lick. She teased that she could see his line from Cleveland to Port Nicollet and all those ports in between. She told herself that she recognized a big talker like the one her mother ran off with when the children were thirteen, twelve, and eleven. But he did have a pocketful of payday, and he took her down Beacon Avenue, to the Top Hat, to the Shanghai.

The simple Cleveland boy took her dancing, more like hoofing cuckoldry, since he pleaded bad pegs and watched her dance with anyone who asked. She *was* Miss Hollywood. He watched. He dosed her rum fizz. That's what Faith, and Honor, guessed later. The Cleveland boy with the money roll gave the Collins glass a stir with his finger and slid it across the table to Faith when she returned to their booth. Here's your Mickey, Miss Hollywood.

Dancing with others.

The fog.

Fighting the boy off as the fog lifted, so slowly. A clearing in Iron Point Park, in the woods that edged the lake, pines the dark teeth of Lake Superior. The dead hoofer with the money roll. No matter. He had his baggy houndstooth trousers down around his ankles, his member poking from between the flapping white shirttails. Her free hand latched onto what it could and she cracked his head with a dead tree limb. He dropped like a hundred pounds of burlapped russets.

The Cleveland boy's collapse surprised Faith, like a scene out of a Hollywood murder mystery. Ida Lupino as Faith. Would Ida's character leave the dead boy in the woods? Maybe, maybe not. This Miss Hollywood considered, going home to her sister. Honor would know what to do.

* * *

Honor asked questions, mostly centering on why this young man. Faith shaded it at first, talking Ida Lupino and all those tough movies, and then, that it just happened, he drugged her and she saved herself. "And, maybe if mama…"

Honor looked at her. The man who long ago passed through town. Mama fell in with him. Then she was gone. Honor understood. Their port city had a great number who passed on through.

Faith and Honor, they fell asleep to Artie Shaw and his orchestra performing "Frenesí"—*frenesí*, Spanish for frenzy. But if there was frenzy in Artie's song, it was of an upbeat and swinging sort. And that is how Honor, with Faith's assistance, took up the additional work that came her way.

* * *

There was a ready supply.

The dapper salesman from Milwaukee. Honor met him at the Shanghai. He with the stiffened johnson that she could only compare to a sawed-off Louisville Slugger tenting his baggy trouser leg.

She laughed when he pressed himself against her, pressed her up to the butcher shop's brick wall, the narrow space between buildings. "There's no goddammed way I'm letting you try to slip *that* into me."

There was a ready supply. Honor and Faith lived in a port city on the Great Lakes.

Sketchy men and fresh-faced boys. Salesmen. Able-bodied seamen. New to town, on business. Off the boats, in port to take on grain or lumber. Always passing through.

Faith attracted the whey-faced youngsters, soft-spoken, away from home for the very first time, such quietly predaceous young men.

The sisters took care of what Honor called "this load of bad boys." There was a ready market for the ground meat and pulverized bone.

* * *

The pigs devoured the slop, snouts noisy, boisterous in the mix, the boar and two sows shouldering one another at the trough, roughhousing after they had grunted down their own.

Abigail slapped playfully at the tough Duroc rumps with her straw hat and told Honor and Faith, "Thanks, girls. Haul in more when you've got it." Her loveliness bending in age and the hog-raising way of life to the look and manner of the actress Marjorie Main.

The Ford panel truck climbed the double-rut road from the scrub ravine that was Abigail's property, up through the gray industrial light, the hog farm a nothing barrier to the Quonset-hutted shipyard directly north, boats in drydock, and the brown-timbered ore docks off to the east, and Honor pointed the truck home, to the flat above the butcher shop.

"Girls," the older woman called, "Give my regards to your kid brother." She smiled at them, the brim of her hat shading her eyes, a vague passing wonder at where they could have scraped up the excess they supplied her with. She shook her head, shrugged. Still. Honor butchered her hogs. It was business.

Honor looked back and waved from the open driver side window, nodded her assent. Nels continued his basic training at Camp McCoy.

"Why didn't she let the piglets out?" Faith asked.

"Their parents like meat so much," Honor said, chuckling. "They would've eaten those piggies right up."

* * *

The day she received the marriage proposal from the man twenty years her junior was the day she found out about his family. The day did not go well for Abigail.

The Western Union telegram from Nels arrived after dusk and the forty-two-year-old woman read it, read his words a second time, out loud, and then she danced around her kitchen, rattling the canned goods stored in the rickety Hoosier, vibraphoning the cooking utensils hanging on the wall. Abigail happily pulled out a roasting pan and considered dancing up the street with it, pounding on the bottom with a tenderizing mallet. Her personal shivaree.

Nels was coming home on leave after basic training and would accept her *Yes* at that time. They would wed before he shipped out for Fort Ord in California.

"Ha!" She knew what she would do. Abigail left the roasting pan and mallet behind. The butcher shop would have closed hours ago, but she wanted to go upstairs, to Honor and Faith's flat. She would celebrate with her future sisters-in-law.

* * *

Abigail danced up the zigzag spine of wooden steps hanging on the back of the Lunds' building, but she stopped on her way, seeing a light from the butcher shop leaking over a curtain rod and through a cracked and torn shade. Abigail tapped the window glass and peered in. Her revulsion teetered her back, nearly off the stairs, and over the railing into the hardscrabble patch of backyard.

In the fluorescent tube-lit shop, sweat-browed Honor glanced up, the hacksaw sliding to a halt in the shoulder of a body. An adult man's body. Abigail shook her head, started back down the stairs. Honor waited for her at the butcher shop's open back door.

"No. No, no, no," Abigail said, attempting to wheel by, skirt her future sister-in-law, and return to—what?—to get away.

"Come in, Abigail." Honor smiled, wiping her hands down her bloodied apron. The scent of iron was in the air. "I'd like to talk to you. About this." She gestured with a slick hand, inviting her to step in. Abigail stood still, frozen, so Honor took her by the arm. Although the former opera singer was a larger, possibly stronger woman, the butcher's grip pulled her directly into the abattoir of onetime gentlemen callers.

The new tube lighting lit the scene all too well: white walls splashed with red, tiled floor and runners greasy with blood, blood, gouts of blood, the puddles clotting to a black rust.

A lighter, piercing scream drowned out Abigail's hoarse cry. She turned to see Miss Hollywood, and, for one last odd moment, Abigail thought of Ted Williams, the Red Sox's Splendid Splinter, as Faith swung the meat cleaver, swung for the fences.

* * *

The South Shore Flyer pulled into the Port Nicollet depot from Camp McCoy and Private Nels Lund climbed off, all smiles, nodding at the conductor, hoping to see his ladylove waving to him from the crowd. Instead, his sisters cut their way through the other greeters on the platform.

After hugging Honor and Faith, Nels said, "Not that I don't think the world of you two, but I was hoping Abs would've been here."

Faith shoved him on the shoulder, smirked, and turned away.

Honor put her arms around her brother and said, "Let's go to the farm."

The absence of Abigail's outsize personality, even with Honor and Faith sitting with Nels at her table, hollowed out her kitchen. His sisters hadn't seen him cry since he was a child, dirt-and-rock burned from a bicycle crash in a back alley, and now he pinched the bridge of his nose, but still the tears came down.

"It takes a man to cry," Honor said. "Go right ahead, hon."

He shook his head. "She never said anything. I must've scared her off with my telegram. Dammit. I told her, wrote to her that she would say yes to my marriage proposal."

Honor put her arm over his shoulders. "Now, we don't know anything about that at all. She didn't bring that up. Did she, Faithie?" Faith nodded, that's right. "All we know is, she heard from some, what did she call it, an opera impresario in New York, or San Francisco, one or the other. And this fellow wanted, no, he needed her in a big production. Only Abigail fit the bill as far as he was concerned. All these years later, since he'd last seen her on stage, she was the one."

"You were going to get married?" Faith asked.

Nels said, "Yes. I wanted to, anyway."

"I don't know what to say, except, like what Honor said. Abigail signed the hog farm over to us, but I have to say, something was burning in her."

Honor agreed.

"Abigail just up and left Port Nicollet"—she glanced at Honor—"In a, what would you call it, Honor?"

"A frenzy. She left in a frenzy."

Then Private Lund sobbed. Love. He had lost it, but at least—he grabbed hold of their hands—he had Honor and Faith.

Closing Time at Mom's

More than once, Jimmy LaCoursiere's tire chains saved the DeSoto from a slippery carom on Duluth's west end streets. He knew where it was, but with the physicality of the weather he moved at a crawl, looking for the neon, the perceived warmth.

He found a space a block away, bulldozed the snow, and parked. Cassie had said, *Mom's Diner, let's meet there at bar time.*

Cassie asked Jimmy to drive up from St. Paul. That was the plan.

He stomped his shoes, knocking off the snow, brushed the heavy flakes from his blue overcoat, felt the weight in his pocket, and looked for her. The diner was loopy with everybody there from the neighborhood's emptied taverns, everybody who didn't have a tippling house to go to, or a whiskey-dicked assignation.

He claimed a stool at the counter and watched her work on her own. The last time he'd seen her was a year ago last summer at the reunion in St. Paul. She was a cushiony fireplug of a woman, red hair regularly washed with peroxide. She was someone he'd never minded pushing up against. In fact, he'd wanted to marry her.

He smiled and caught her eye. She looked surprised to see him, but he knew it was a put-on. That was okay. Flipping her green pad to the next slip, her eyes darted back at the swinging door to the kitchen before she asked, "What can I get for you?" And lower, "I didn't think you'd come."

"Hey, Cassie."

"Come on. Lot of people waiting." Then she looked at him, blue eyes pleading. Her voice a whisper that could drive him crazy now weaved with fear. "Come on, Jimmy. Come on, baby."

He blushed at her urging him on and she smiled, looking down, remembering. The moment snapped when the cook called her name from the pass-through window. She tightened up. Jimmy said, "Coffee, black, you know, and a burger, fried onions."

She scribbled in her pad and hurried off to take another order.

The cook had to be the one.

When there was any slowdown, taking orders, pouring coffee, clattering plates of greasy food in front of people, the cook barked from the window. Cassie would lay the orders down on the window ledge and he would snatch them up, mumbling when she was near. Once, he came through the door and really gave her the business. He had a gaunt, craggy face, reminded Jimmy of the actor Robert Ryan, down to those dark eyes locked into a too-many-mile stare. Jimmy wanted to drag him in back and brain him with the bottom of a hot cast-iron skillet.

When she brought his burger and coffee, she nodded, *That's him. Dunphy.* Jimmy remembered what she'd told him on the phone: *None of us wants to be alone with him. He blocks any of us girls in the storage room. Yanks up our skirts. There's nothing we can do.*

Jimmy asked, "You?"

There's nothing we can do. The others quit. I want to, but first I wanna teach him.

13

I want a gun.

Dunphy burst from the kitchen again and grabbed Cassie's upper arm and hauled her into the kitchen. Jimmy heard the muffled shouts.

When she came back out, he could see the impression of Dunphy's hand on her arm.

He'd heard enough. He'd seen enough. Jimmy pulled the weight from his pocket, the Colt Detective Special. He asked Cassie for a doggie bag. When she brought it and turned away, he said, "Wait. This is what you wanted." He slipped the gun into the bag, slid it across the counter.

The minutes before closing dragged. Dunphy never let up, though it was coming and he didn't even know it.

The winter storm blew itself out. The regulars, gabbed out, dream broken, stirred themselves to move and emptied out of Mom's into the snowdrift streets.

Dunphy came out and motioned at Jimmy, *You. On your way. It's closing time.*

The cook didn't even know what was coming. Jimmy thought he did. He loved Cassie all the more for it.

His sister.

His hot kid sister.

But then she turned and aimed the gun at him.

Payday Friday

He met her the first time at Otto's. Payday Friday, he wanted to meet her again. A date he'd call it. A short drive from the plant after showering, slap on the bay rum. "Someone's getting some tonight?" He grinned, blushed. Anders shrugged, a young twenty-five. She wouldn't expect him.

The wind barreled off Lake Superior, greasing the iron footbridge high over the railroad tracks with ice. A perilous walk to the lot where his Starlight coupe sat. He'd tuned it up just before winter clapped down. She'd get a cozy ride home. Anders was mindful in some respects.

Otto's, red and yellow neon over the front door, snow ghosts blowing past the streetlights, hunkered down in the chiaroscuro of moonlight, streetlight, snow, and the wooden railroad trestle running out to the harbor and docks.

Anders looked around, pulling off his stocking cap and lined choppers, unzipping the heavy red-and-black plaid jacket. Somebody had plugged the Wurlitzer with coin. Patsy Cline sang "Walkin' After Midnight." He looked for Marcella's Lucille Ball–red head. In that booth? No.

He ordered a sip and snort from Raymond and slammed home the warming shot. "Say, you seen Marcella tonight?"

Playing dim, wiping glasses clean with a dingy cloth, Raymond twitched his melon head no.

"Marcella Lundquist?" Anders tried again, post-Fitger's sip.

Raymond cocked his head. Anders knew he was nowhere near a halfwit. What, did he have to slip him a sawbuck for information, like he was a movie detective? "That leggy redhead?"

Anders smiled. "Yeah. That's Marcella. So?"

"No. I don't think so."

"What?"

"But I just came on at six." The Hamm's clock on the wall read 11:18. "Not to say she wasn't here earlier. Uncle Otto was tending bar then. He'd know. But he's probably sleeping now."

Nodding, Anders swept the barroom again. Three couples slow dancing. No Marcella. He turned back. "Set me up. I'll be right back."

He hit the john. Stomach wobbles. He situated himself on the throne just in time.

Belly settled, he noticed an expensive cigar-brown over-coat hanging from the door. Anders checked its pockets, looking for some identification. Leather gloves, a pack of cigarettes, a matchbook, and an envelope with First National Bank printed in the upper left corner. It was thick with cash.

After splashing water on his face at the sink, drying off, he pulled the envelope out of his pocket. Opened it again, thumbed the bills.

He glanced at the door latch. Locked. He pulled the wad out, counted it, then he recounted it. He looked in the mottled mirror. He wasn't dreaming. He counted the bills a third time.

Each time, the figure was the same.

Ten thousand dollars. More than he made in two years.

He shoved the envelope inside his shirt, tucked low beneath his belt. He walked back to the bar and pulled on his jacket.

Raymond, at the end of the bar, gestured come over. He wouldn't look Anders in the eye. "Okay. I saw Marcella. I saw her leave."

"Yeah?"

Raymond polished a slice of bar top real estate. "Yeah, she was talking with Mr. High-Life. Hinckley, the bank VP." The name meant nothing to Anders. 'Bank' did. "They were getting hot and heavy in a booth back there. Fucking redheads. Even that one, what you seen when you came in."

"Okay?"

"They left like they were going to make Hot Springs tonight." Raymond rolled his eyes. "The dick-for-brains didn't even wear his overcoat. He's probably hopping her in his car right this minute."

"What's he drive?"

"Aw, kid. You don't want—"

"I'm not going to do anything to him."

Raymond shook his head. "A big fucking Caddy. Shiny, black. This year's model."

The wind still blew. Anders spotted the banker's '56 Cadillac in the lot. It stood out. It glared.

He walked alongside, his shadow not falling across either occupant. High-Life, eyes closed, leaned back in his seat. Marcella's head dipped in his lap like a drinking bird toy.

Anders moved off into the trestle's dark shadow, a hand in his coat pocket pressing against the ten thousand.

The Cadillac action dropped off.

Anders walked to his coupe, figuring, the three of them, they each got their payday.

Taste Your Lips of Wine

Rick Odegaard and his kid brother, Frank, sat in the Ore Dock Tavern at Fifth and Calumet, three blocks south of State Highway 2, on the backside of noon on a sweltering August Saturday in 1958, when the already soused Rick began to slide, skinny ass over teakettle, from the padded red vinyl of his barstool, declaring, "I would walk off a goddamn pier—"

Frank caught him by the elbow and the bartender, Johnny Patzau, smiled. The Odegaard brothers were well-practiced, graceful as modern dancers in street clothes.

Rick concluded his do-or-die statement of purpose as the wobble and roll ceased. It was as if nothing had interrupted him. "—and drown in the bay for my mother."

"Our mother," Frank said. He had been drinking icy Northern drafts, two or three.

The older brother raised a finger, twirled it, for Johnny behind the bar. Another Black Velvet. Neat. "I would do it for her, even before I'd do it for Naddie." Rick's wife, Nadine. He slapped the bar.

Frank covered his glass with his hand when Johnny reached for it. Shook his head. His brother would soon be spewing diarrheic gibberish, the signal for Frank to roll him home.

"Drowning in the bay still leaves her empty-handed. Old Man Nord will still send his son around."

Rick agreed. "I swear, I don't know where her bucks go." They go the same place yours go. Frank thought it, didn't say it. He ducked his head and said something that Rick could not pick up.

"Again?"

Frank sighed, shook his head. "There's this place I go by on my route. Okay?" Rick gave the high sign. "Place outside of Hurley, in the woods." Frank's whisper—he's considered the joint often, heard of its existence from the brotherhood of truckers, only spoke of it to one other person, someone who could help, a second gun. It would solve the problem. Money draining through their ma's sixty-five-year-old fingers like it did. "What I hear, they've got slots and roulette. Women from around town make some money there, too. You know? Cops turn a blind eye."

A vague whisky smile crossed Rick's thirty-eight-year-old puffed, pink face. It had been a long time. The memory of it: making love with Naddie when he was home on leave. That's all they did until he stepped back on the train. But then he gave Frank a stern look. "You go there? Park your truck out front? Get some young ass?" Johnny Patzau passed, wiping down the bar, whistling the Everly Brothers hit from earlier in the year, "All I Have to Do Is Dream." Rick's abrupt slap to his brother's head was a sorry failure, but he was otherwise clear. "South Shore will have you out on your ass if you're caught screwing on their dime."

Frank drove delivery—regular stops at diners, bars, resorts—throughout northern Wisconsin for South Shore Wholesale Foods, Inc. "Fuck's sake, they won't. Anyway, what I have in mind, we'll need a car."

"A car? You don't have one. Naddie's got her Chev, but she'd say no fucking way. 'To drive to a whorehouse?' No."

"We'll need a dependable car. Nadine's Bel Air. To get out there and get the fuck away."

Rick arrived at his half state, watchful before the fall, and then the sudden slipping, unaware, into the blackout stream. "Away? Away from what?"

Frank softly said it. "From Sylvia's Hideaway, the place I'm talking about. Listen, listen. After we hit it. With what we can pull, Ma won't have to worry about Old Man Nord or his goddamn kid for a good long while."

Rick blinked, but it was as if he agreed. "Naddie's car."

To himself, the kid brother added, *And your service revolver.*

* * *

Frank gathered in one arm the hundred-thirty-five-pound bag of potatoes that was Rick, slapped a generous tip on the bar with his free hand, gave a nod to Johnny Patzau.

Johnny smiled, dropped the money into the tip glass behind the bar. "Wait, I'll give you a ride."

Frank was tempted, knowing that it would be hotter than fuck all else on the streets of Port Nicollet. But it would be all the more so sitting inside Johnny's car, even with the windows rolled down. Instead of yes, he said, "No. Thanks. I got him."

It was a three-block walk east on Fifth Street to Rick and Nadine's paint-flaked clapboard duplex that stood a half block south of the shipyard. Frank wanted to get in at the shipyard, had a go, but he and the hot rivets did not get along—would've paid better than South Shore, that's for sure. One good thing was meeting Johnny Patzau. Johnny didn't make the cut either. But now it was the hot afternoon and people gawped from their porches. Anything counted as entertainment. Frank stumblebummed his brother along. He flipped them off when they stared too long. Old Man

Nord cackled like a crow from behind his porch railing, old Arco Coffee can for hawked chaw at the side of his rocker. "Rick's looking like the ghost of your old man." Frank told him to stick it. Their old man died in '53. Ma had a taste for the stuff now, probably did for a long time.

* * *

Nadine, a nurse at the TB sanatorium weekdays in Duluth, was hanging laundry on the line in the backyard, hair up in a babushka, wearing a sleeveless cotton top and faded purple pedal pushers. Barefoot on the dandelion lawn. She saw Frank hustle Rick up the wooden stairs to the apartment on the first floor, pulled a clothespin from her mouth, and called out, "I'll be right in to give you a hand, Frankie."

He nodded, knowing she'd try, but hoped she wouldn't bother. When he had Rick settled in bed, his snoring like the terrific buzz and cut of a lumber mill's circular saw, Frank stepped over to the chest of drawers and pulled one open, reached in under Rick's rolled black dress socks and underwear and ran his hand over the barrel and cylinder of the .45. Rick had a second gun that he'd mentioned when he was honorably discharged after twenty years, one with an eight-round magazine, but, patting around, Frank couldn't find it.

The edge of a drawn shade tapped and he turned. Nadine called for him from down the hall. Frank paused, then went to her, like a schoolboy who would pay when he reached the principal's office.

The first time with her was on the screened-in back porch in June. Afternoon. Always, it turned out, after they poured Rick—veteran of Europe, the Pacific, Korea, more scars in than out—into bed. Nadine had walked Frank out onto the back porch, and she told him, the afternoon sun white hot, a green humming through the elm leaves, scent of lilac, the buzzing of bees, the silence of the butterflies in the weedy garden outside the screen door and down the steps, she told him this the first time she finished him off, "When I blow a man, he stays blown."

She said this as she wiped her lower lip with a curved index finger. She licked it clean. Nadine eyed Frank and he returned the look, tucking himself back into his dungarees, zipping the opening closed. He returned the look intently and smiled. It was because he pictured someone else kneeling in front of him. He absolutely thought of someone else.

* * *

That night, the Ore Dock was filled with jukebox melodies spun at forty-five revolutions per minute, Saturday night persuasion patter, the clink of bottles and glasses, men and women imbibing to smooth the path to bed, the backseat of a car, to whatever space was available. Frank knew the course wasn't as open for people like him.

He sat at the end of the bar. He'd figured himself out a year ago, at twenty-seven. What the fuck had he been doing with his life? His mind spun. Frank had gone so far as to check the law, went to the Carnegie Library in downtown Port Nicollet. By state statutes, his was a sexual perversion or deviancy. Fuck them. Frank felt fearless. He drank the Northern longnecks that Johnny slid his way while the bartender appeared to nurse a single beer all evening. "Watch out," Johnny Patzau said. "I might be trying to get you drunk."

* * *

Frank exited the tavern by the backdoor, into the alley where the Mercury Eight coupe was parked at a slight remove from the other vehicles. The car was old, a '46, but cherry, and he climbed past the front passenger seat to the leatherette upholstery of the backseat and waited, stretched out, his eyes peering through the car's rear side window. The alley was dark except for one bare light bulb thrust out over the tavern's door, lighting the red brick wall, the dented trash cans all in a row. Frank waited for closing time, waited, handling himself, hardening, waiting.

A figure finally emerged and made for the car, joined Frank on the backseat, and exclaimed, "Hello, big boy."

"Aw, Johnny," Frank chuckled roughly.

"What, big boy? What?"

"What took you so fucking long?"

* * *

The two lounged, panting at either end of the backseat. Johnny wiped himself dry with a tail of his sweat-dampened white shirt. Frank, pants and boxers down around one ankle, looked him in the eye, heart rate slowly returning to normal.

"Well, she's a good runner," Johnny said, patting his car, pride in ownership. "And if Nadine nixed it from her end."

"Rick had it nailed. She thought I'd be out chasing strange quiff."

Johnny's grunt built to a laugh. "I know what you really like, baby."

"That's right," he nodded. "You up for it?"

Johnny smirked. "Give me a minute."

"No. Come on."

"Of course, baby. Say the word."

That clinched it for Frank. And there was something else, looking across at Johnny in the dim alley light filtering into the backseat space of the Mercury. They could take the money for themselves. Leave this town, all of it. All of them. Leave it all behind.

They heard the rumble of a car start up and then pull away, down the alley, but paid it no mind.

* * *

It was nightfall when the two men rolled into the dirt parking lot fronting Sylvia's Hideaway. Johnny, behind the wheel, gave the lot the once-over, then said, "Quiet. I mean, I've never been here. But doesn't it look quiet to you, baby?"

Another car turned in and parked on the other side of the lot. Frank heard its tires and counted it with those already there. He didn't know if it was quiet or not. He'd never been inside. Frank shrugged and said, "It'll be good. It'll be good." A squeeze and a kiss and they climbed from Johnny's Mercury Eight.

Later, they would realize that as a couple they shared a two-minds, one-thought sensibility. That night, Frank and Johnny walked through the door, glanced at each other, and thought as one, *Fuck, no masks.* They went with it, viewed as odd ducks by everybody at Sylvia's Hideaway, patron or employee. Johnny improvised his conception of a well-heeled duffer up from Minneapolis, a Remington shotgun hidden beneath a moth-eaten blue overcoat, and Frank, as he was in any new situation, wide-eyed and reserved, not uncomfortable, but alert, a .45 in the pocket of his out-of-season jacket. Frank and Johnny may have looked out of their element—the overcoat and jacket when the temperature was still in the high seventies—but they took in the place. There was no hiding.

Women sat at round café tables lining the wall at one side of the long room. These daytime waitresses, laundry workers, housekeepers, farmers' daughters, housewives—some from as far away as the Twin Ports to the west and Iron River to the northeast in the Upper Peninsula, the others homegrown—gave a passing glance to the newcomers and smiled, but who they were waiting for were the boys they really knew, the boys they really liked, the ones who'd paid and paid well in the past: doctors and dentists, bankers, judges and lawyers. The women nursed weak tea drinks. Three hiked their hemlines up ever so slightly, honey for these newcomer bees. One couple, a zaftig, frizz-haired woman in steel-rimmed glasses and a longshoreman strayed from his Lake Superior port, danced cheek to cheek to a slow number by Sinatra that played on the Seeburg. She whispered in her partner's ear and he pulled back, quick to blush, then grinned, leaning in again.

A wide, rounded archway opened up to a back room where Frank saw someone on an obvious losing streak at roulette, the wheel operated by a stick of a fellow who looked like Percy Kilbride, albeit bent, of Ma and Pa Kettle fame.

A scrawny woman in her fifties tended the bar opposite the working women. She had a sly drift to her strabismus-afflicted eye that said she'd seen more than anyone would ever care to see, and a hint of a vicious streak like Frank's Aunt Harlean, his ma's sister, whose slap to the back of the head when he and Rick were kids was a no-warnings-given crack of the whip.

Aunt Harlean's double smiled and Frank's wariness increased twofold. "Good evening, boys. I'm Sylvia. Take your coats off and name your pleasure."

Two women abandoned their table and moved to acquaint themselves with Frank and Johnny, moved with the heightened artlessness of those practiced at the trade, at least of those who spent their daytime hours waiting tables, making lunch for their children, nursing their babies, and pleasuring, tired or not, their boyfriends and husbands.

Sylvia's sliding eye fixed on the two men unswayed by her girls. "Take off your coats, boys," she said. She laid a maple baseball bat across the bar, her muscled forearm tattooed with a man-of-war. Gray stubble rode her upper lip that curled in a smile that was not a smile. The dancers' song ended and they drifted off to the side.

In the seconds of quiet between singles, the Hideaway's door slammed open and everyone flinched each in their own human way: The working women chirruped like a forest's cloud of birds; Sylvia screamed, "Fuck," Pa said, "What?" and the roulette-losing gambler soiled himself. Another customer, fresh from the john, scattered his many chips across the blood-red linoleum floor. And they all faced the front door, Johnny backing to the bar, Frank to the opposite wall.

It was Nadine. And she waved Rick's missing pistol, the Colt with the eight-round magazine. "You dirty—" She stabbed the barrel at Frank.

"Aw, goddammit," Sylvia whined.

The Pa Kettle lookalike, he casually put his hands behind his back and said, "Well, isn't this a fine how-de-do." Then he brought a piece forward that looked too heavy for him to hold and point with any ease or accuracy, an assumption Frank felt deeply wrong. Pa knew what he was doing.

Sylvia gripped the bat just above the knob, but she didn't lift it up.

The next record dropped in the jukebox. The Everly Brothers. Johnny grinned and shook his head.

"What in the green-eyed hell do you think you're doing?" Sylvia demanded of Nadine.

Frank's mind pinballed and he looked across the room at Johnny. Johnny shook his head, said, "Baby, I didn't bargain for this." He carefully laid the Remington 870 down and toed it off to the center of the room. Frank whistled, something of a despairing warble, and did the same with his weapon. They'd watched enough *Dragnet* and *Highway Patrol* on Ma Odegaard's Du Mont television set. They'd seen all the TV westerns, too. They were happy to have the weapons nowhere near them.

Nadine shrieked in recognition when she saw the revolver skate across the floor.

"Must I ask you again?" This time, the muscles in her arm flexed and she tapped the slugger on the bar, wood on wood.

Nadine's gun hand dropped.

The cannon at the opposite end of the room didn't waver. Pa was steady. "What would you like me to do, Syl? Could hold her all night." He gave a nasty laugh.

"What do you want, gun moll? You want Jerry here to blow you back out the front door?"

Pa—Jerry, as Sylvia called him—had the grin of a ravenous jack-o'-lantern.

Sylvia said with disgust, "Oh, leave your pistol on the floor there and get the hell out of my establishment."

Frank and Johnny watched, relieved, as Nadine did exactly that, not backing out but turning and running.

"Bang," Jerry barked. He laughed at his joke. "What about these two?"

"These two nancy boys." Sylvia pursed her mustached lips. The Everly Brothers' hit faded out. No one got up to plug the box with more coin. "These two'd be in a load of trouble, don't you think?"

Jerry nodded.

Sylvia looked at Johnny, then Frank. "We have our quarterly raid coming up tonight, boys. Sheriff's department, some police." She checked the watch clipped to the flat bosom of her drab housedress. "Boys like you, you wouldn't like the county lockup."

Jerry agreed. "It's a little 'we scratch your back, you scratch ours.' Every once in a while, they attempt to clean up. For the papers, understand. But you two? In jail?" He whistled forlornly.

Frank said, "We understand. Could you just, um, lower that gun of yours?"

Jerry smiled and, like the corners of his mouth, the pistol remained up and on them.

"Couple of chuckleheaded virgin bandits, you two," Sylvia said. "Leave the shotgun and the forty-five where they are. Get your asses out of here. Out back. Climb out the goddamn window and go back from where you came."

* * *

Sylvia's backdoor was nailed shut. She apparently didn't like surprise entrances from the rear of the building or nonpaying absconders. Frank and Johnny left by the window. They ran and stumbled through the dark woods until they finally decided it was safe to walk, angling their way back to the highway to hitchhike back to Port Nicollet.

"She was right. What a couple of bandits we turned out to be," Johnny laughed. "More like the Haynes sisters in *White Christmas*, giving the slip to the sheriff in Florida."

Frank threw an arm around Johnny, pulled him away from the road and down to the ground. They rolled, kissing hard, near merging, one into the other.

Afterward, the two men skinny-dipped in a lake down in the woods, mosquitos be damned. Frank and Johnny held each other, neck deep in the water.

"You're good with that?"

"I want you to be happy, baby."

The next afternoon found the two on the road, the Mercury Eight regained, U.S. 61 in front of them. They were moving to the Twin Cities and beyond, leaving their covert lives in small-town Wisconsin behind.

* * *

Afterword

Rick Odegaard, to the wonder of everyone he ever knew, stopped drinking, cold turkey, no assistance from AA or any other group. He stopped. The width of his backyard, a gravel alley, and another backyard, his mother's, separated Rick and Nadine, but never divorce. Rick died in 2000, stone sober and nodding in a recliner, watching the History Channel.

Nadine lived across the alley from her husband with Ma Odegaard, caring for the old woman who might very well have lived forever, until she died a week after her hundredth birthday. Nadine's senile dementia diagnosis followed closely on Ma Odegaard's death. Rick had her admitted to a care center in Duluth. She may be living there still.

Frank and Johnny left Port Nicollet and the Odegaard family behind in the late summer of 1958, settling first in Minneapolis. In the mid-sixties, they relocated to San Francisco, even farther from their roots. At Bay Area parties, they were known as the couple with the outrageous tale about a long-ago caper in the Midwest. They had tried robbing a rural Wisconsin casino and brothel, a fully illegal enterprise, and failed. No one could believe it. Frank and Johnny? Desperados? The two men told the story for years. Their friends laughed until tears ran down their faces.

Johnny died in the mid-nineties, a heart attack, and Frank had him buried in Colma, the City of the Silent. One day, a bereft Frank looked around and found that everyone he used to know was gone. He returned to his roots in the Upper Midwest and passed in 2005.

Sukiyaki

I wasn't a window-peeping perv, but that was how I first saw her. Lucia and I had moved uptown from Superior's North End in the summer of 1963. It was the final piece that my mother and assorted family friends needed to be convinced. I was guilty of overreach. I had married a Greenwich Village painter and then brought this bride of mine home to Wisconsin. Now, after living a month in a flat at 5th and Weeks, we had moved to a house uptown. I accepted a position as an English Lit lecturer at the state university and our new home was within walking distance of the campus. The North-Enders, they were sure that I'd forgotten where I'd come from, the old neighborhood with the first and second generations of Scandinavian-American stock, willfully ignorant, unambitious. I was an academic, an ambitious one, and I wasn't a window-peeping perv.

It was mid-June and we'd lived uptown less than a week. The humidity was something awful that night and our one-year-old, Marky, couldn't get to sleep, so I took him for a walk. Really, I just carried him through the quiet night of our new neighborhood. He knocked off in no time, a diapered, sweating heap against my shoulder, but I continued walking, smoking one KOOL after another, the rubber soles of my sneakers padding down the sidewalk, noting who was still up, who was not, the screened windows open to the still night. Returning home by way of the gravel alley that cut through the block, I noticed a light on at the house across the alley from ours. The shade was partially open. Framed in that letterbox of yellow light were her bare shoulders and breasts as she dried herself off with a white towel. Less than twenty feet away. I looked around, but, of course, no one else was out, and I crunched up to a tall lilac that edged the alley, watched her through its branches, and lit another cigarette. I watched until she finished, flicked off the light, and left the room, Marky never waking at my shoulder. Hurrying home, I put my young son to bed and woke Lucia in our own.

* * *

The neighbor across the alley wasn't part of the neighborhood welcome group. That association consisted of old, white- and blue-haired women who stopped by during the day to introduce themselves to Lucia, distracting my boho wife from her latest canvas, dropping off fruit baskets, offering to watch Marky because they knew how young couples needed time alone—a dinner date at the Hi-35 Supper Club, a movie at the Beacon or Palace—and to gossip about everyone else in the neighborhood like old biddies are wont to do.

Lucia laughed while she told me. "They really look down on the Albrechts. The hubby, Phil, is some grizzled World War II vet, ten or fifteen years older than Margo, the wife. No kids and"—she glanced at my can of Hamm's and the lit KOOL—"drinkers and chain smokers."

"The idea."

"Indeed. I think they wanted to say more about Margo, but couldn't bring themselves to say the words."

"What? Harlot? Trollop? Tart?"

Lucia slapped my arm playfully. "The hints were flying fast and furious, let me tell you. The ladies sort of lost me though

31

when they started going on about this Margo Albrecht's looks. How did Mrs. Ellis put it? Margo has 'coarse north country features that aren't much to look at in broad daylight.' I thought that was pretty mean."

"Is she enticing their old husbands? The tramp."

"Search me. But I wanted to invite them to dinner. Phil and Margo. They sound much more interesting than Mrs. Ellis's crowd."

"Where do they live?"

"Across the alley from us. Imagine that, the cradle robbing veteran and his homely tramp of a wife."

"Across the alley?"

"Yes, the green house. I walked over this afternoon, but another neighbor lady—Mrs. Hooker, can you believe that? Mrs. Hooker said that Margo works in the strip mall on Belknap, by Red Owl. She manages a liquor store."

At that point, recalling the bared shoulders and breasts, I was catching little of what Lucia was saying, but was cognizant enough to offer to invite the Albrechts over. "What do you say? Saturday night?"

"You'll go do that? You're an angel!"

Finishing a smoke, I glanced up and down the alley. Neighborhood kids were plowing through the gravel on their bicycles, fathers were firing up lawnmowers in backyards, while others were just pulling in from work. Then I looked across the alley at the Albrecht house. Someone was at a rear window but was gone as soon as she saw me staring back at her. That's what I thought, anyway. I smiled, stubbed out my smoke in the gravel, and walked over to meet Margo Albrecht. I wasn't feeling angelic.

"Come on in," a woman called when I knuckled the wood frame of the screen door. It was a voice rubbed down to its essentials.

32

The kitchen was dimly lit, the afternoon sunlight coming in through the window over the sink. She was at the counter, prepping for supper, or a cocktail, wearing a man's gray and blue plaid robe. It was too large for her, but the hipshot way she stood there with her back to me brought out the round swell of her backside. "Mrs. Albrecht?"

"Margo," she said, glancing over her shoulder, and then she slowly spun around, a paring knife in her hand.

My breath caught somewhere near the top of my chest. She had tied the too large robe smartly at her waist, yet it gaped above the tight knot. The subdued light and shadow revealed curve and heft. I wanted to draw my fingers down in a straight line from her throat to her belly.

"No, really, call me Margo." She made no move to close the top of the robe. "I always change out of my clothes as soon as I get home from work, so excuse the robe."

Remembering to inhale and exhale with some measure of normality, I said, "No apology necessary." Then I introduced myself and explained why I had dropped by.

"Ah, the young professor. We'd be happy to come over on Saturday." She called for her husband and he walked into the kitchen, shirtless and wearing baggy Army fatigues, the evening newspaper in his hand. Phil was a short, leather-faced man, muscular, but sickly looking at the same time.

He shook my hand, giving the impression of one who couldn't be bothered, and so left me alone once again with his wife.

"So, Saturday," I said.

She came up and touched my lips with the hand that wasn't holding the knife. I didn't smell food on her fingers. I smelled her. "Yes." Margo thumped me playfully on the chest. "Saturday." She let her fingertips linger. "Hard." Then they slid down.

I was flummoxed. "I work out a little at the university gym."
"I believe it."
"Saturday?"
"Saturday."
I took a cold shower when I got back home.

* * *

Lucia and I learned a lot about the Albrechts when they came over for dinner. Phil, the banty rooster Kraut, enjoyed his Grain Belt beer—he walked over with a case of the swill—and a lit Marlboro was never far from his hand. His voice was on the rocks, a cocktail of beer and smokes, and I needed only to feed the occasional single word question for him to go on about his years as a Seabee in the South Pacific.

All the while that Phil had my ear about the Seabees, or the city streets department where he was a working manager, my eyes were on Margo. She lounged on the sofa across the living room from us and spoke with Lucia. Certainly, I assumed she had been a tease from the day she learned the sway accommodating quiff held over men. But, while Mrs. Blue Hair was right in that Margo's coarse North Country features were not much to look at in broad daylight, or lamplight, I didn't necessarily want her in any light.

We played 45s on the record player and Margo loved the hit from Japan, "Sukiyaki," playing it over and over again. She and I danced, and to dance so close to that woman was to receive the promise of her voluptuosity. After a second slow dance, her eyes widened. "Hm, I believe you have a hard-on," she whispered.

I let her go and stepped back, unsure if I'd heard her correctly. When I was about to ask, there was a bellow, as if from a dying animal, from another part of the house.

Shooting a glance at Lucia, she responded with a shrug, her arms spread.

"That's Phil in the john. He's sick, really sick." That is how we learned that Phil Albrecht had an aggressive form of cancer. He had just begun his chemotherapy treatments that week. Margo sipped her beer. "Sometimes he sounds like a big, old dog that's gotten its tail slammed in a door." She rolled her eyes. Lucia and I didn't know where to look. "Lucky he's one tough son of a bitch."

* * *

My office on campus was eight blocks from home and that summer I would walk to and from work. Most afternoons I would hear "Sukiyaki" coming from their place. *I shall walk looking up.* Was that the translation? It was something like that. Or, *Tears fall from my eyes as I walk alone.*

Crossing over to say hello, I would find Margo sunning on the back porch. Her oiled thighs would slide against each other, a greeting that slipped into my blood. Other days, she would be pulling down her sun-dried laundry from the clothesline, her arms reaching up to pull loose the wooden clothespins, breasts taut against her white linen blouse. I wanted to clasp her from behind.

* * *

The Albrechts invited us throughout that summer to their cabin on Little Pickerel Lake. We would go, but we never spent the night, forget any Friday through Sunday debauch. The place was a slapdash three-room affair ideal for deer hunters and fishermen that Phil and his brothers, who lived up and down the shoreline, built in one weekend in the early fifties. Lucia and I would spend a few hours with the Albrechts, Phil, Margo, and I knocking back brown long-necks, and then when I, with our hosts, was fairly snockered, Lucia would drive us back to Superior. Lovely Lucia, driving and fuming the whole way, and Marky squalling in the backseat. That I recall anyway. It became routine.

I have no clear understanding why I treated Lucia so poorly. She was nothing if not good and loyal to the core, attractive in a way different from other women in 1963. She was a Jackie-Kennedy-as-boho-painter with jet-black hair, magically transferred from New York City to Superior, always vaguely bewildered as to how that change had occurred. Her curiosity charged her eyes, her art, and her daily commentary on goings-on in North End and uptown. I have no clear understanding why I treated her this way—the horn on for Mrs. Margo Albrecht—beyond the usual male curse: opportunity.

The penultimate trip to Little Pickerel Lake consisted of Lucia on the beach with her oils, brushes, canvas and easel, Marky playing in the wet sand, leashed to his mother's waist, Phil on the sofa, on the nod with a copy of *Field & Stream* on his chest, and Margo and I, dancing.

I moved across the cabin's swaying floor with her, again to the bouncy and sad Japanese pop song. She ground her sweet spot against my thigh. I snuck looks at Lucia out the cabin's picture window. She worked her canvas down by the shore, Marky at her bare feet filling a red bucket with sand. My hand angled into my dance partner's blouse, into her bra, and fished out her breast.

I kissed the prize while Phil sawed a winter's worth of logs. Opportunity.

* * *

Three days later, Phil invited us to watch him kill and skin a pair of rabbits. Margo called us over for dinner and the slaughter was part of the full experience. Lucia eyed Phil's martial chop to the neck of each rabbit, then the peeling away of the skin, the butchering. She didn't flinch. I thought it was brutal, the oddest thing I had ever been asked to witness.

* * *

I tried to break it off with her, put out what had been smol-dering. Leaving the office early, and Phil still at work, I went to their place. I had a plan. I knew what I was going to say. She could take the example of our dancing at the cabin for how messed up it was: Lucia outside with Marky, painting the Little Pickerel waterscape, Margo's husband crapped out on the sofa while I pawed at her. It had to end. The trouble was, the moment I saw her I was hard.

She glanced down. "Are you going to let that go to waste?"

I shook my head. She wasn't listening. As I turned to leave, Margo caught my arm and pulled me close, kissing me, firmly palming me.

I grabbed her by the shoulders but it was she who maneuvered us backward, bumping into chairs, doorframes, knocking against a table, into her bedroom and onto the chenille spread of the bed.

* * *

Before she let me go, she said, "The next time you're fucking Lucia, think of me."

* * *

It was still early when I got out to the cabin. I'd driven out on my own the Friday before the fall semester began with the idea of making it up to both of them. Phil was drinking coffee that looked like motor oil and Margo was exercising in front of a small television set to *The Jack LaLanne Show*. The signal from Duluth shifted from snow flurries to a full-on blizzard.

I was not a fisherman and Phil knew that, but I had always been a gregarious, go-along-to-get-along guy. When he said, "Let's go out on Little Pickerel and pull in some crappies," I agreed.

There was a layer of haze that the sun saturated with gold. I could see his brothers in the middle distance on both sides as we slid the boat across the sand and out onto the lake. I could see them nod in recognition.

Out on Little Pickerel, we sat and fished. I did anyway, poorly. Phil, the poor son of a bitch, the cancer killing him by fluctuating degrees, some days better than others, smoked and, I felt, studied me.

"That was some time when you were out here last. Boy-oh." He laughed.

I shook my head. "Yeah, and I had a hell of a time getting to work the next day. Preparing for fall. Would've been happy if my head had just exploded and been done with it."

"Shit, yeah." His brothers sat in their boats, smoking their cigarettes and Dutch Masters. "Ask you something?"

"Shoot."

"Did you fuck her?"

I turned and looked at him and had the presence of mind not to ask when. "What?"

"I want to know if you put it to Margo. Did you fuck a dying man's wife right in front of him? Because the last thing I remember was the two of you dancing and you grabbing hold of her pods."

"Christ, Phil. I wouldn't do that." I focused on the fishing rod, the line looped out into the Little Pickerel chops.

There was a whoosh and then crushing pain and, yes, I saw stars, I saw the whole view from the planetarium's front row seat. My arms flew out and he clubbed me again. He tumbled me into Little Pickerel Lake.

My face bobbed inches below the lake's ruddy surface. He leaned over the side of the boat, refracted through the water into a shifting, melting figure looking at me. The figure vomited, his own death pocking the surface of the lake, and I was gone.

Long Ago on a Sunday in June

They found the body in the field of tall dun weeds between Speedway Avenue and the high chain-link fence of Hackberry Petroleum. The space, empty until then, was a brownfield before that word's first use in the era of environmental protection. The body lay on the ground in a stiff fetal curl, a plaid shirt tugged over the head, three white buttons missing, threads frayed. One ant crawled up and over a pale cheek and then continued over an open eye. The uniformed policeman had to turn away.

* * *

The end of his day would be a loud chirr, a roaring susurrus, sand pouring through a sieve, granules draining into total quiet. Or perhaps the grind was the car's tires as it pulled away.

Now, morning. And his mother.

She looked in at the door, a tall, gray ghost though she was young, in her thirties. She told him, "Honey, time to get up."

He was already awake. Sunday. Why? Two thick, wire-bound bundles of newspaper, bringing the national and local news to Port Nicollet, along with the latest in sports, or the only sport that mattered to him, baseball, the Minnesota Twins—there hadn't been a major league baseball team in Wisconsin since the Braves left for Atlanta—the entertainment section with the TV paper pullout, a brief rundown of the week's episodes of *The Man from U.N.C.L.E.* and

Mission: Impossible, summer repeats, but still his favorite shows; the comics section that he hadn't paid attention to in years; and the crap sales and ad supplements. The two bound stacks, pitched between four-thirty and five from the back of the Tribune's Chev panel truck to the southeast corner of the blacktopped playground behind Roosevelt Elementary, waited for the snip and release from the wire binding. The boy would load the papers into the wagon and then trundle them off for delivery.

Patrick Severson stretched, delayed getting up. She peeked in again. "Do you want cocoa and toast? I'll get it ready for you, if you do."

"No, thanks. I'll get something." He continued to laze.

"Patrick."

"Okay. I'm getting up."

His younger brothers, Tommy and Richie, shared the lower bunk bed. They will have imprecise memories in future years. *Get up already so we can sleep.* Did one or the other yell that at Patrick?

A Sunday morning in June, dark yet, edging toward daybreak, sunrise arriving closer to five-thirty. His mother whispered, "See you later, honey. Remember. The Sveden House or Dominic's Pizza tonight. Your choice." His birthday was coming up in three days. On June 29, he would be fifteen years old.

"Go back to bed, mom." She will remember these words.

Patrick adjusted his underwear. He had an erection, so he didn't want her in the room when he climbed out of the top bunk. He's fourteen—again, almost fifteen for cripe's sake. It was bad enough he had to share a room with Tommy and Richie. His sister, Kim, had a small room all to herself.

He thought he might like to disappear someday. That dry, slipping sound from when he was just waking. He would like to go like that, sand funneled away to nothing. He thought he'd die at twelve. Stupid game he had: If I can't hold my breath through this commercial break during Saturday morning cartoons, just this once, I will die when I turn twelve. The commercial ended; *Tennessee Tuxedo* returned. He survived. Stupid and senseless, he'd been a goofy eleven-year-old.

Patrick knew he'd wear the short-sleeved shirt and blue jeans with the cuffs rolled up an inch or two—his mother said he'd grow into them. Not that he'd laid the clothing out the night before like Kim would. He knew he could snag them in the dark. But he was the older brother. He turned on the light and his little brothers, in memory, snarled and moaned. He kicked the side of their bed. "Shut up, you guys." Turning off the light, he left the shared bedroom without looking back.

In the kitchen, Patrick flipped the light switch, the round fluorescent tubes moth-shuddered to full brilliance, one after another, and went to the refrigerator. Bridgeman's chocolate milk in a glass bottle. White bread from the Red Owl bakery. It was his summer version of fall and winter's hot cocoa and toast that his mom offered to make for him. He turned on the radio, tuned in a Duluth station. "Wouldn't It Be Nice" was playing. When it ended, he flipped the dial but only found Lutheran church programs with triumphal organ music. He turned off the radio while pouring a glass of chocolate milk. Church had never been stressed in the Severson home. His dad was sailing on the Great Lakes most of the year, he had no time for pastors; his mother gave up long ago on sending any of her children to Sunday School, or Patrick to Wednesday afterschool confirmation classes. The pastor's wife was probably happy that he no longer showed up for those church basement sessions, because he had questions she could never fully answer. Why had there been a Hitler? Why was President Kennedy assassinated? Why did God allow this awful shit to happen? Not that he asked her in those exact words. Patrick left the rail-thin woman frazzled. In the end, he no longer wanted her inconclusive answers.

He ate at the kitchen table, dipping a folded slice of unbuttered bread into the cold chocolate milk. Kim was disgusted by it, but he didn't care. For a little crunch, he ate handfuls of Tommy and Richie's Cap'n Crunch straight from the box, some of the small yellow squares falling to the table, bouncing to the floor, leaving a trace of Patrick. Their old dog, Muff, would have been there to snap the cereal up midair, but mom had him put to sleep last fall. Distemper. The dog's absence crushed Patrick. He still teared up.

Leaving the house, he slammed the paneled door, rattling its loose, square windowpane. He rattled the knob, the door shut tight. His mom would appreciate that even though it remained unlocked. Patrick would never know the day, coming soon, when Port Nicollet neighbors slept behind locked doors. The wood-framed screen door slapped behind him. He walked the tilted porch floorboards, the dark green paint worn and peeling, to the wooden steps, then down into the backyard. The grass. He swore under his breath, looking from side to side as he approached the garage. The grass was getting long. He should have pushed the reel lawn mower through it on Saturday, but instead he'd gone to Duluth with his friend Joey Maki and Joey's dad for a ballgame. The Seversons' yard was small and wouldn't take a half hour to mow, but the chore would intrude on plans he and Joey had for this Sunday.

The garage was cool and dark and it would remain so that humid day. He'd thought of grabbing a sweatshirt on his way out of the house, but decided it wouldn't be necessary. His parents' '65 silvery sky-blue Plymouth Belvedere took up most of the space so his old Radio Flyer hung from a nail on the wall by its chipped black handle. He lifted the wagon down and, after grabbing the wire cutters from his dad's workbench, brought it out to the narrow backyard walk. Then he began the short trek to Roosevelt Elementary and the newspaper bundles. The wagon wheels tumbled down the cracked city sidewalk with a sound the Lake Superior agates made when his dad tumbled them in the polisher. The wheels rang out loud in his ears, louder than the early birds driving the few blocks east on Port Nicollet's main drag, Beacon Avenue, out for coffee and breakfast, or the graveyard shift from the hospital, the oil refinery, crawling home to bed.

After Patrick finished up with his paper route, the day with Joey would be pretty much seat-of-the-pants. He would go home and eat an early lunch, bologna on white bread with French's mustard, a glass of milk, or, if his mom wasn't around, a sugary glass of instant iced tea or a bottle of Royal Crown Cola. After lunch, he and Joey would either listen to the Twins-Tigers game on the radio or watch it on TV at Joey's house. His family had a color television set, a Curtis Mathis. The Seversons still had a black-and-white model in a blonde wood cabinet with doors—doors, on a TV—something handed down from Patrick's Grandma Severson after Uncle Gene bought her a portable color TV. It was embarrassing. But the Makis had the color set now and Mr. Maki would let them watch it as long as they promised not to screw around with the color and fine-tuning knobs.

Patrick thought of Marla Maki, Joey's sister. She was a year ahead of them in school. If a kid believed what the

articles said in his mom's women's magazines, and Patrick
did, no question, girls were lightyears ahead of boys. Intel-
lectually and emotionally. Sexually. Marla was a year older,
so a year plus lightyears older. He was screwed. Correct that,
he shook his head, he'd *never* do it. It would never be with
Marla. Patrick couldn't see it. She might be ahead of him a
year *plus* lightyears, but a girl like her, no, she would never
think of doing it. The only thing that Patrick had going
in his favor was that, according to Joey, Marla didn't have
a steady boyfriend. There was hope. Patrick could dream.
And he did.

A few blocks to Roosevelt's playground, and the empty
wagon continued its pots-and-pans racket. Patrick expected
it to wake the entire sleeping neighborhood. But there was
only this one old guy. Mr. Pope. Elliot Pope. He yelled from
his porch for Patrick to "knock it the fuck off, or I'll fix your
wagon." That was last Sunday. Brother. Yelling *fuck* out loud,
outside. His dad only swore like that at his workbench,
and Patrick knew what *fix your wagon* meant. He thought
about turning sixteen *next* year and getting a real job. He
didn't want to waste money buying a new wagon. He was
going to be fifteen in a few days, for cripe's sake. He tried
it out under his breath—*Fifteen. Fucking. Years. Old.*—and
laughed. He wanted to grow up. He wanted to go to high
school. He wanted to *maybe* more seriously try cigarettes.
Lucky Strikes. Uncle Gene's brand.

His birthday, three days away. He hoped he would get
the Beach Boys' *Pet Sounds* from his mom, and, okay, his
dad, who wouldn't remember his birthday anyway, off somewhere on Lake Michigan or unloading taconite pellets in
Detroit. Or was it Ashtabula? Mark, the clerk at Wahlstrom's
Music, was playing the album in the store after its release

last month. If Patrick didn't get the album for his birthday, he would have to buy it. There was no way around it. He listened to the whole album twice, three times, at the music store, and he felt it summed up his life at fourteen, going on fifteen. He heard "Wouldn't It Be Nice" and pictured Marla, standing in front of him. Always Marla. He would have to play the album on the family's stereo console in the living room. When mom, Kim, Tommy, and Richie went shopping in Duluth, they would be gone for hours, he could turn the stereo way up high. But the living room stereo console, that would only go on until he saved enough cash for a portable stereo from Montgomery Ward. His mom could order it for him at the catalog store downtown, next door to Wahlstrom's Music.

The old man, Pope, was on his front porch in a red robe and, just like every Sunday, drinking coffee, smoking a cigarette, and watching for him. Patrick could see his shining bald head from a block away and thought of crossing to the other side of the street. Instead, he slowed his pace, steered the wagon around the worst of the cracks and shifts in the pavement, thinking that would lessen the noise.

"It's not working," Pope shouted. His wrinkled face was red. "Watch it, watch it, don't roll that rattletrap on my property, goddammit!"

Patrick froze, one worn wagon wheel on Pope's edged lawn. At least the old man didn't come running off the porch. The paperboy rolled on.

Pope laughed, shook his head. "For being such a pain in the ass, you should give me a free newspaper every Sunday." Pope's was the last newspaper he delivered every Sunday morning.

Patrick didn't look back. He didn't want to see him again if he could help it. The old man was never around when he pitched the paper onto his porch. Next week, like any fourteen- , fifteen-year-old boy, making plans, he would cut around, wide of Pope's side of the block, and avoid the old man entirely when he started out in the morning.

His thoughts turned to food, where to have his birthday dinner. The Sveden House or Dominic's Pizza? Joey was coming with. At the Sveden House, a smorgasbord, a cafeteria-style restaurant, Patrick's favorites were the baked ham, macaroni and cheese, and baked beans, all laid out with a pleasing shine under the warming lights. There were so many other tempting dishes to choose from, pushing your tray down the line, loading your plate, loading it like it was going to be your last meal. For instance, Joey and spaghetti and meatballs. Patrick remembered last year, when Joey brought a heaping plate of spaghetti back to the table, the Seversons all teased that they couldn't see him. Patrick's mom began singing, "On top of spaghetti, all covered with cheese, I lost my poor meatball when somebody sneezed. It rolled off the table and onto the floor and then my poor meatball rolled out of the door—" His mom's singing. Patrick had laughed so hard.

That was the smorgasbord restaurant. Good food and lots of it. But, then again, he was turning fifteen and the place attracted so many old people sitting around with other old people, older than any of his grandparents, and his grandparents were in their sixties and seventies, but these people, dressed for church, sat gumming their mashed potatoes, had their Salisbury steak cut into itty-bitty pieces and fed to them by their gray-haired children. They dribbled gravy down their clothes, although they had napkins tucked in at their necks. For tonight, Patrick leaned toward Dominic's, the best pizza in town, with the Michael Bukoski mural of the Port Nicollet waterfront stretching from the shop's front door to its rear exit. He wanted to get into Mr. Bukoski's art class when he entered Port Nicollet High in September. That was a given.

The pizza shop was downtown on the city's main drag, with booths to eat at and the pizzamakers up front, three high school- and college-age guys in white paper garrison caps, white shirts, white pants, and bibbed white aprons, working behind a clear plastic barrier. Customers could watch as they rolled out the dough and spread it on the flour-dusted wooden pizza paddles, spinning the white disks as they crimped the edges with their fingers, then ladled on the red sauce—newer pizzamakers splotched themselves rookie-style with the sauce that was much better than the canned pre-seasoned tomato sauce that his mom used when she made pizza at home with sliced hot dogs—wiping hands on their aprons, and adding the ordered ingredients. They slid the pizzas into the wide-mouthed ovens and let them bake, checking them, reaching in with the paddle and rotating each with care so that they baked evenly. That's the job Patrick wanted when he moved on from his paper route. Pizzamaker.

What did Patrick look forward to at Dominic's? Pepperoni pizza. Coca-Cola. Bonita Weir. The food that he believed he would indeed have to grow to fully appreciate, because at fourteen and younger, he liked the pizza and pop, but they did not like him. He had to grow into the spicy heat of the pepperoni placed generously on top of the mozzarella cheese and the bubbling pizza sauce. The Coke? The acidity always felt like it was going to eat up his entire stomach lining. Royal Crown was like water in contrast.

Then there was Bonita Weir. Bonita Weir was his mom's friend and she worked in the back, in the pizza shop's kitchen. Dominic Prestigiacomo's family entrusted her with Dominic's ground beef seasoning recipe. After browning, Bonita dumped the ground beef into the kitchen's restaurant grade mixing bowl, where she spooned in the secret, measured portions of garlic and onion powder, the other unknown herbs, and then blended the mixture to create magic, or, at least, Patrick's favorite pizza topping. His mom said Bonita treated the ground beef recipe like it was the instruction manual for building a hydrogen bomb. Even when she thought she'd figured out each ingredient and how much to use, she wouldn't try it out on at-home pizzas. Hesitant, she said, "Not just yet." She stuck with the hot dog pizza and the store-bought sauce. She continued with it for years because she thought the bland bologna flavor, with the canned sauce and prepackaged grated cheese, was Patrick's favorite.

Bonita Weir. For Patrick, it was not just that she knew her way around a tub of ground beef mixed with mysterious spices and herbs. No. When the Seversons lived on the northside of Port Nicollet, the old neighborhood, when he was a little kid, a baby, Bonita would occasionally babysit him. She was loud in every possible way: perfumes and clothing colors that announced her entrance in advance, flashily dyed hair bubbled up in a bouffant, cool-jeweled cat eye glasses, the constant fog of cigarette smoke, her startlingly space-piercing voice and earthshaking laugh. She lived loud, his dad liked to say. Another of his dad's descriptions? One that he had told Patrick's mom and wasn't meant for his ears: "She's a cocktease, sure. But she never does anything."

Patrick's mom asked, "And did you test her out on that point?" Whispered words. His dad didn't respond. He had to pack because he was shipping out the next day.

Bonita Weir was a cocktease.

In the last year, two years, almost, since the age of thirteen, she liked to give Patrick hugs when she would see him. He was a small guy for his age, he knew that. Bonita would pull him to her and press his face between her breasts, the perfume at her cleavage, soft and firm and all one sensation. He would squirm as though he was saving himself from suffocation. His intent, maybe a little bit, was to make his mom think he didn't like it, that it was embarrassing. It was embarrassing, but he enjoyed that embrace, that closeness to Bonita Weir, so much so that his former babysitter and his mom's old friend, she had to be twenty years older, sometimes her touch, her scent whirled in his horny mind—yes, Mom, horny—with the same feelings he had for Marla Maki. In his most private moments, this blend of Marla Maki and Bonita Weir was heavenly.

Roosevelt Elementary edged into view. The wheels of the wagon clanged round and round. He started breathing again. He surprised himself. It was like he'd been holding his breath while holding his own with these converging, fired-up thoughts of piling on the baked ham, macaroni and cheese, working as a Dominic's pizzamaker, eating pepperoni pizza, drinking Coca Cola, idolizing Marla Maki, and jacking off, yes, jacking off to Bonita Weir. In his mind, the song began to play on repeat: "Wouldn't It Be Nice."

He pulled the empty wagon up the sidewalk incline, up from the corner to the westside doors of the school, the yellow and black civil defense sign posted above the double doors, and then down to the rear, behind the fifty-year-old red brick building. The blacktop playground: where the teachers parked during the school year, where the hopscotch and foursquare courts were painted onto the blacktop with chalky white paint, where two basketball hoops with raggedy, snapped chain nets stood guard on either side of the gymnasium doors, where they stood guard, but not for Patrick. The blacktop playground that Patrick Severson would disappear from, long ago, on a Sunday morning in June.

The wagon clattered as he pulled it across the blacktop. He was a slight fourteen-year-old boy who had been mistaken for being younger. He knew where he was going. The burn barrel, a rusty metal drum, and the two bundles of the Sunday newspaper on the southeastern corner of the Roosevelt Elementary School and playground block.

Patrick bent over the newsprint bundles. Robins were singing. It was going to be a beautiful day. He didn't mind humidity. Heat and humidity. That *meant* summer on the south shore of Lake Superior. He could hear the traffic as it continued to build. He could hear one car, louder than the others, maybe speeding, peeling out from a stop sign.

Snipping the thick wires from each bundle, he hoisted the newspapers into his wagon.

Patrick carefully lifted the front end of the wagon and pulled it off the curb and into the street. Then he saw the car that came to a stop.

A window rolled down.

He ducked his head and squinted into the car's shadows. Curious, he smiled.

Much of the neighborhood slept on, slept in on that long-ago Sunday morning in June, in houses a street- and yard-width away, houses where parents slept and where their children slept, and where each and every one of them thought they were safe. And further away, they slept.

His brothers and sister and mother. His father on a Great Lakes ship.

Aunts, uncles, and grandparents.

Friends.

Teachers.

The police.

The detectives.

And yet, while they slept, Patrick Severson ducked his head and squinted into the shadows.

And, curious, he smiled.

Far from Home

He caught the bug while at Marquette, track and field, class of '53. Evenings now, the lanky man runs the up-and-down of Iron Point Drive, running before it becomes a health fad, long before Jim Fixx and *Running Magazine*. Iron Point Drive is not uninhabited, although it has that look and feel. He mentioned this aspect to Patti. The long, curving band of weather-pocked blacktop, it won't see improvement until 1973, winds through the woods, edging the city park it shares its name with, the park's rocky shore jutting into Lake Superior, taking the brunt of the lake's weather. Tucked into the woods are nine homes. The evening jogger knows them. He knows many things about this city and can separate its gossip from its facts. If asked, he recalls that the Iron Point Drive homes were built not too long ago, in 1959 and 1960. Architectural ramblers with a Scandinavian bent and too expensive for most people living in this working-class city. Hell, he works for the city and he can't afford one. Not to say he wouldn't like to. He admitted as much to Patti the other night. The developer moved on to the Twin Cities in 1961.

The pine and paper birch woods along the drive are filled with the echoing chirrups of the birds settling in for the night. *Here's where I am. Where are you?* That mass song blends with the rubber slap of his basketball shoes until both are smothered by the roar of an engine. It approaches from behind and he stands off to the side of the road as the car sweeps around the curve. A new model going too god-damn fast. What's the name? Like a Mustang fastback that has been pulled from either end, stretched out. Two-tone, red and black. Something ugly that will never last. He just has time to read the plate number, shakes his head. He'll call it in later. A Marlin, that's it. He is a cop. Blomfeldt is a detective.

Chet Blomfeldt steps back onto the blacktop and continues his run, his mind passing from room to room, the fair starting up in a week, it's already being built, the city overloaded with carnies, *carny creeps* they call them at the station, his kids, Kenny, Barbara, Rita, and John, all wanting to go and, of course, at different times, but that's his wife's domain. Close that door. Opening another, he thinks about Patti with the gap between her two front teeth. He smiles, gets hard.

She's pregnant. She told him last night and he was calm. She expected more. McElmurray would say Blomfeldt was being his imperturbable self. Blomfeldt is thirty-five and this will be his fifth kid. He asked Patti about school, wouldn't this play hell with her plans. She is going for her master's in the education program at the state teachers college.

Her eyes searched his face for a clue. That's right. She expected more. Not finding anything, not happiness, not apprehension, not finding anything other than the face of Blomfeldt the cop, she said, "Well, there is the option of having it taken care of."

Blomfeldt's self-possession, what he needs for his job, fractured. Just slightly, but it fractured. "No, honey." He shook his head.

"What do you propose then?"

He didn't respond. She had him there. She knew someone who knew someone who could do it in South End.

"It's dangerous," he said. "It's illegal." He recognized how lame it sounded as soon as the words left his mouth.

She had this way with her left eyebrow. The Lift, he called it. And there it was. She could ask the question again. *What do you propose?* But she didn't have to. It hung in the air like a thought bubble in one of the Sunday comic strips that he read to his kids.

Blomfeldt was the one who could look into things, get the answers. Normally. Not last night. "Ah, Patti."

* * *

Another car, a Ford Galaxy, pulls up and rolls along at his pace. A plaid elbow hangs from the open window and a heavy-lidded young man gapes out while keeping an eye on the road. Leon McElmurray, Blomfeldt's partner, a rookie in the investigations unit. "I stopped by the house. She said you went for a run. And—voilà!"

He came to himself. The moment. Real life. He stopped and bent over, hands on his knees, panting. "What's up, Leon?" He stands and stretches, pulls a pack of Luckies from the pocket of his sweats.

"A body just off Speedway Avenue, near the refinery."

Detective Blomfeldt sucks in the smoke from the burning tobacco.

"You heard that missing person report? The fourteen-year-old kid? Severson? Uniform patrol thinks it's him."

Blomfeldt nodded his head. The noise of the goodnight birds grew louder.

"Well, let's go, Big Dad. These bad guys aren't going to catch themselves."

* * *

54

They drove by Chet's so he could change out of the gray sweats, take a quick shower. Patti on his mind. That door hadn't closed all the way. Donna comes in and gives him a kiss, reaches for him, says the kids want to stay up for the late show on Channel 10. It's Sunday, a summer night. "I've got to get ready for work, Don." A dead teenager off Speedway Avenue. Patti considering a visit to a doctor in South End.

McElmurray runs interference downstairs while the Blomfeldts are upstairs. The kids love the young detective's synopsis of the last sci-fi movie he saw, the pulp novel he is currently reading. The girls scream. The boys laugh. All mouths hang open, but they are hungry for more. Kenny, Barbara, Rita, and John will all live long though not necessarily healthy lives, high cholesterol, heart disease, alcoholism. But sociopaths will not murder them. They will be teachers, an engineer, and an academic who will live their lives. But they will live out their lives largely away from this city.

Donna never asks when Chet expects to be back. That stopped once she understood the job, especially after the promotion.

He is quiet and is about to slip past, kissing her on the cheek. Donna takes him by the hand. "Wait," she says, and reaches up with her lips.

"We've got to get going."

She glances toward the stairs.

Blomfeldt leaves his wife by their bedroom door, off to join his partner. And Donna, she calls out, "Bye, Chet. See you, Mac." She is her own detective. Something of her husband's profession has rubbed off after all these years.

* * *

Blomfeldt stands in a field near the oil refinery, his nose doubly irritated, the dandelion puffs and the oil processing stink. The holding tanks. The tower lights popping on now at dusk. The smoke stacks, their plumes drifting straight up, no breeze. Uniformed cops mill about, a couple of squad cars pulled into the field off Speedway, his and McElmurray's unmarked on the avenue, lights turning.

His oldest son, Kenny, is about this boy's age. The difference is that he will grow up. He will be an engineer in the petroleum industry, relatively wealthy, absolutely distant. This boy, the dead boy, is slight, apparently easily broken, curled up on the ground, an inverted S. Kenny said that the squad car lights reminded him a little bit of the fair. The fair and *The Twilight Zone.*

The boy's plaid, short-sleeved shirt is tugged taut over his head. Blomfeldt stands over the body and turns slowly, a vane caught in the barely perceptible breeze that has just come up off the lake, cutting the heat and the humidity. McElmurray with a solitary drop of sweat rolling down the right side of his face asks, "What is it?"

Blomfeldt turns. The murder didn't happen here, not in this open field. He takes in Speedway Avenue in both directions. It would have been a private act.

"What is it, Big Dad?"

It is the most at ease that Blomfeldt has been all day. His mind is operating outside of himself, far away from the many rooms, away from the first family and the second family. Focused on the dead boy who is farther from home than any of them.

He walks off to the unmarked car and McElmurray follows, saying, "Okay. Let's roll."

The Ballad of John Rider

The flight was under four minutes, a trick of levitation at eleven at night, up Market Street and then Portola Drive to Diamond Heights. Jefferson Airplane's "Have You Seen the Saucers." With the opening notes, the cabdriver reached over to the dashboard and turned up the FM station's volume. When the song concluded on its sci-fi buzz and fade, he glanced at me in the rearview mirror and said, "Welcome to San Francisco."

It was 1974 and I was eighteen. I'd arrived in the city via a Greyhound Ameripass, and while that cross-country trip had its own disparate misadventures—a collection of stories connected by only, I admit now, a naïve young man from Wisconsin set loose on the modern American West—it was San Francisco that I was aimed for all along, and my aim was true. I thought I might even remain in the city, blow off my freshman year of college that fall. I would get a job and stay.

"Pete?" My Uncle Eric expected me at his apartment. But not that night. His eyes were bloodshot and fractured, and I knew that familiar funk of weed, recognized the artist who created the music chiming from his living room. "Pete"—stepping aside, welcoming me in—"*Jethro*, I didn't think you'd arrive until, what, next week."

I walked in, shrugged the rucksack from my shoulder Jack Kerouac style, and ignored the "Jethro" nickname Eric tagged me with years before, because whining would have been pointless. Bullheaded. He was a Strom and I was a Strom. If he was going to call me by *The Beverly Hillbillies'* nephew's name, so be it.

We stepped down into the hexagonal living room, lights turned low, sticks of sandalwood incense smoldering on the fireplace mantle. A jeans and chambray shirt-clad young man with unruly hair and beard reclined on one of the two Victorian sofas, a Hindenburg-size joint in his hand, the zeppelin's tip smoking.

"This is Duncan," Eric said. "Duncan, this is Jethro."

"Pete," I corrected, and Duncan nodded, offering me the burning airship.

"He's my nephew, Duncan. *Verstehen sie?*" Eric spent the Korean War in Germany and phrases he had picked up remained over twenty years later. "He's just out of high school."

Duncan said, "Sorry, man," diverting the joint midflight to Eric. I recalled the disaster newsreel's sobbing reporter: *Oh, the humanity.*

I did manage to suck in a deep breath of the quality smoke that floated across the room. In my small hometown, low quality pot was the expectation. Whatever Eric and Duncan were indulging in was a treat. And the music. That was too. The reel-to-reel tape rolled on playback. "Is this who I think it is?"

Duncan's face lit up, bowled over at the possibility a kid from a little Midwestern town might know, but before he could say anything, Eric forestalled him, a lift of his hand. "Who do you think it is?"

"John Rider." No confirmation necessary. It was John Rider, I knew it. I'd been buying his albums for five years at that point, my older brother even longer. Rider released his debut LP, the psychedelic *Colors in My Garden*, in sixty-seven, after Lennon and McCartney, Brian Jones, and Syd Barrett applied their wash of aural color. "John Rider," I repeated, adding, "*Recluse* Rider," because that's what the music rags had dubbed him.

Eric winced at "Recluse," shook his head, while Duncan's weed-enhanced titter budded through the room.

"Anyway, that's what Lester Bangs calls him in *Creem*. But this is great, Eric. I've never heard it before."

My uncle said, "That's because, I shit you not, it's John Rider's latest." He glanced at Duncan, then back at me. "Keep it under your hat."

I never thought to ask that night if I could see the tape reel's box, the artwork and photography, the lyric sheet, the list of musicians playing on each song. Music is magic, and this was musical mesmerization: ringing twelve-string guitars, Baroque noodling with harpsichord, hill country dulcimer, juke joint piano, rumbling electric bass, spare drum work, and spacey synthesizer.

"Sonic harmonics." That's what Duncan called the mix. Leaving at sunrise, he shook my hand. "You've heard John's new nickname, right?"

"No."

"Reckless. Not Recluse. Reckless. Remember that, okay?"

I nodded as Eric took Duncan by the shoulders and pointed him out the door.

* * *

The Ameripass was a great deal for an eighteen-year-old off on his own, although stuck at the Sioux Falls YMCA my first night out—the depot closed, no departures till morning—I wanted to turn back, be homeward bound. But I continued on the next morning. The pass was a wide-open, ninety-nine-day ticket to ride anywhere Greyhound rolled in the lower forty-eight. You could disappear in America. The company's TV spokesman was Fred MacMurray in the guise of the *My Three Sons* dad, a gosh-by-golly barker encouraging people to see America from a relaxing seat on the bus. The price was low. How could I say no?

After that first night in San Francisco, listening to John Rider's new music and cracking Eric and Duncan up with stories of my antics on the road, I was ready to ball up the paper ticket and chuck it and my freshman year at Barron County out the window. But I didn't. Instead, I sat on the guest room davenport and considered the Ameripass. I ended up tucking the flimsy ticket away, between the pages of my paperback copy of *On the Road.*

* * *

Eric, two nights later: "I have to run over to my boss's place. Want to come along?"

I jumped at the offer. It would have to beat the previous night. I'd wandered into the city's Tenderloin neighborhood looking for the studio where the Airplane, the Dead, and Crosby, Stills, Nash and Young had recorded. I'd stopped to gawk in the window of a closed leather goods shop and a reflection in the window materialized beside me, a young woman in a flowing cape. She passed me a handbill for Jim Jones and the Peoples Temple— But that's a different story.

When I first met him, Eric's employer consisted of instruments: a Blüthner grand piano—McCartney played one on *Let It Be*; two Martin guitars, six- and twelve-string; and an Epiphone bass, all these in a room overlooking a silent, rolling Pacific.

"Don't touch anything—*especially* the instruments. In fact, just stand where you are," Eric directed, then he left. I couldn't hear him though he worked his way through other parts of the house. Moonlight flooding in through a curved window wall lit the music room. The ocean's breakers rolled in silence.

Tell me *not* to do something. I glanced back. Stepping to the grand piano, I lifted the keyboard lid and played the first nine notes of "Imagine."

"Stop. Just stop." Eric came from behind and moved me away from the Blüthner. He wiped down the keyboard and then, after closing it, the lid.

"Peter"—no Jethro—"It's important that if you want to come with me when I have to work here, that you *listen*. When I tell you not to do something, not touch something, a book, an instrument, a gimcrack, follow my instruction. *Verstehen sie?* I'm not trying to be an asshole. It's just—it's just, this is his home. Not hermetically sealed, but damn close. So, please. Touch nothing."

"Who is he?" The family back in Wisconsin didn't know what Eric did for a living in San Francisco. Yes, they knew what he did when he lived in the Midwest. After serving in the U.S. Army, he'd worked for a while as a steward on a Great Lakes freighter, drove a delivery truck with a Teamster card tucked in his wallet, and at one point he was a laborer, assembling industrial bakery equipment. When he moved to the Bay Area in the early sixties, it was, for the family, out of sight, out of mind. "Who is your mystery employer? Howard Hughes?"

Eric crossed his arms and stared at me, then said, "John Rider."

"What? No, wait. What?"

"John Rider is my, as you have said, *mystery* employer. I'm his— I don't know: right-hand man, gofer. I make things run smoothly for him and his organization."

I grinned, color me dumbfounded. All I could think to ask? "Can you turn on a light in here?" I wanted to see the music room's instruments under the bright lights.

"No." He sized up the room. "So, now I've gotten the place ready for his return. We should get going."

Backpedaling to Eric's Fiat, I took in John Rider's home, call it a mansion, snapping it for my mental photo album, like I would Abbey Road Studios, Wally Heider Studios in the Tenderloin, or the Jefferson Airplane House on Fulton Street.

As he drove us back to Diamond Heights, I apologized for touching the piano. Some might say it was over the top, but the apology led to another question. "How about Duncan? Does he do what you do?"

I caught the swell of a laugh on Eric's face, but he didn't let it break. "Oh, not Duncan. No."

"You're his boss? I mean, you kind of marched him out of your apartment the other night."

Eric let that slide. "Let's listen to that new Rider tape when we get back to my place. I'll probably give you what's left of my weed too. It's been playing hell with my allergies. Just"—zipping his lips—"no word to your mom and dad."

* * *

The next day I pretty much obliterated by smoking a grass zeppelin on my own, then letting a wild hair spring me out of my vegetative sofa state and out the apartment door. I trekked, no, floated up and down the hills of San Francisco in that stoned condition. By midafternoon, I was on Mount Sutro and I couldn't find my way back to the apartment.

A man in a red Jaguar convertible picked me up on Crestmont, I think it was Crestmont. He offered me a beer from the cooler stash tucked between the Jag's bucket seats. I whined like a twelve-year-old: "Thanks, but I just need a ride to my uncle's place." There was the sudden braking action at the curb and he reached over and popped open my door.

I was still on Mount Sutro, thinking I could see the Diamond Heights neighborhood, its curving rows of fifties shoebox duplexes, from whatever street I was walking on. A Karmann Ghia painted British racing green pulled up. I didn't have high hopes.

"Give you a lift?" It was Duncan, looking over the lenses of his mirrored aviators. "Peter? Not Jethro, right?" he asked as he pulled out into traffic.

"What the hell are you doing up here? Getting a better view of Sutro Tower? It's not even up here." He laughed, took us on a few hairpin turns. "I heard you were with Eric at the house the other night."

All my coiled astonishment sprang out. "Holy crap, man! Yes. Like, was I stoked, absolutely—"

Duncan nodded, signaled with the cigarette in his hand that we could move on from the initial blown away perspective. "Did Eric mention me?"

I thought back. "No. Yes. I'd asked him if you did what he did. What your role was."

"Yes?"

"He ignored me."

Duncan laughed joylessly. "Nothing—oh, why should I ask you— Okay, nothing about me, about what I do? What I've done?"

"No."

He pulled into a Safeway parking lot, a spot tight against the public sidewalk. We weren't going grocery shopping.

"I came back from L.A. that night with John Rider. Later. The same night you were there with Eric. He didn't mention we were coming in?"

"No."

"Reckless, man. He's a mess."

Reckless. Not Recluse. Reckless. Remember that, okay? "Yeah?"

Duncan glanced over at me, then back at the grocery store and the people walking in, walking out, going about their everyday lives. "Yes. Reckless John Rider's burned to a crisp. That cereal? Crispy Critters? He's a bowlful."

My mouth hung open. Duncan smiled, chucked me under the chin to close it. "Okay. But with all the music, the albums—how long?"

He blew a Marlboro stream. "I don't really know, Pete. I was late to the Reckless Rider party. His mind, it's pretty much like I said, man, crunchy cereal. He still has those terrific vocal chops. The cat truly does. But that's it."

A swipe at the dust on the dashboard allowed Duncan time to consider his next words. "The last tape, the one you heard, the new LP? Reckless sang lead, and damn well. Session players played the music, and they did amazing work. Me? I wrote the music and lyrics."

I looked at him and sputtered, "No way."

"Ah, yes."

* * *

He didn't have much money, but Duncan bought us dinner at a Doggie Diner, even treated me to a T-shirt featuring the restaurant's iconic dog, the smiling, bow-tied, red-hot dachshund wearing a chef's hat. He was a worried man, he didn't have to say so and didn't, I could tell that much at eighteen. How long Rider had been the way he was, that was an open question.

Duncan was hired over a year before via a nondescript ad in the back of *Rolling Stone* and a lengthy, puzzling audition: *Do some John Rider for us. Do something John Rider could have composed.* He'd blown away the interview panel that included my uncle. Now, here he was. The record company was releasing the new LP, it could be any day, but Duncan felt at loose ends.

"I haven't been told the release date. Reckless doesn't know. He doesn't really know me, though we've been traveling buddies up and down the coast a number of times. But here's what really puzzles the hell out of me, man: Who wrote and recorded the earlier albums? Where are these talented cats now? Rider's the cash cow, but where have all the old hired hands gone, man? I'd like to know that."

* * *

The next day, Eric left for L.A. He told me he'd be gone for at least three days for meetings with record company execs, working out the logistics for Rider's upcoming release.

I felt him out. "Will there be a tour?" I already knew from *Crawdaddy, Rolling Stone, Creem*, and Duncan that a tour was not in the cards. Reckless Rider hadn't performed live, anywhere, in over three years. The rock magazines, Rider was their cash cow as well, wiped the sweat from their collective brow: *At least John Rider continues to produce music that we can review.*

"Enjoy the city while I'm gone," Eric said. "And stay out of trouble. *Verstehen sie?*"

The first time I'd gone to John Rider's ocean view home, I checked the house number and cross street when my uncle and I left. The second time I went there, I was able to give the cabdriver the approximate address.

At Rider's front door, I wondered if I was the reckless one. What did I expect to gain by showing up and ringing the doorbell that played the first seven notes of Groucho Marx's "Hello, I Must Be Going"? The next steps were easy since no one answered the musical chimes. I could have walked away. Instead, I tried the door. It was unlocked.

It seemed every San Francisco abode I stepped into that summer of seventy-four was socked in with the fog of pot and incense. On this second visit to John Rider's home, I just followed my nose.

The piano bench had been knocked over, a junk drawer's worth of material tumbled from its storage compartment and scattered on the floor. An antique wing chair replaced the bench in front of the piano's keyboard. I recognized John Rider. He sat in the chair, staring at the black and white keys as if they were a curiosity. His elbow rested on an arm of the chair, his hand cradling the side of his head, mouth gaping, his now doughy face frozen in wonder.

"Mr. Rider?"

After few minutes, his head swiveled to take me in, the dazed look of his face unchanged. "John," he said. "Mr. Rider is my father. And my grand. Dad." He took a deep breath from the effort. "John."

"John," I was bummed by his burned-out aspect.

He managed to point a bent finger at me, the fingers of his other hand caught in the long, ratted tangle of his prematurely gray hair. He pointed, tapped in my direction, and finally, with effort, yanked his other hand out of his hair, three fingers encircled with the gray matting, pulled from his scalp, apparently, with no pain. He continued to point at me.

"I'm Peter Strom, Eric's nephew."

He took a breath, a clotted gurgling through his sinuses. "You? In L.A. with me? Last time?"

"No. That must've been Duncan. You know? Duncan?"

He touched his chin. "Beard? Right, man?" He smiled when I nodded. "At least you won't have to worry about that." Rider laughed and, as Uncle Eric would say, I shit you not, I got goose bumps from the musicality of the man's laughter. He did. He still had something.

But still: "What won't I have to worry about?"

He waved me off in slow motion. "The big change out, man. The cosmic disappearance." His hands orchestrated a *poof*, and whatever may have been there was gone.

"Duncan will—you're saying Duncan will disappear."

Rider's hands repeated the poof, slowly, very slowly.

"How?"

Rider was fascinated by the movements of his hands.

"How will Duncan disappear, John?"

"Just gone, baby. Gone, gone, gone"—his knees were crossed and his hands landed there, one atop the other—"like the coda of the song."

* * *

Duncan and I got high listening to the Rider LP on Eric's reel-to-reel. I should say we *tried* getting high, smoking one of his outsized joints. It didn't work. I'd told him about my visit with John Rider.

The tape ran out, the tail flapping round and round until Duncan flipped the lever, turning off the machine. As he put the tape in its box, he sang the old Animals' hit "We Gotta Get Out of This Place."

"You're right, man."

He looked at me. "I've got no bread, Pete. I'm stuck inside of San Francisco with those Reckless John Rider you don't work for me no more blues again. I'm stuck, brother. Stuck. And I've got no idea who I should be on the lookout for— you know? Is it Eric? Reckless Rider? Some hit man"—*hit* man, the musical kind, made him chuckle—"I'm, I don't know. I'm in trouble and I can't get away from it."

That's when I told him about The Cosmic Disappearance. The Poof.

* * *

When Eric returned to San Francisco, he brought back intensity in spades, a hip ferocity, a skull session with Duncan was in order. He phoned the few numbers he could normally reach him at. Nothing.

"Did Duncan stop by at all when I was in L.A.?" His cool a thin layer masking something like anxiety.

I shook my head, playing at youthful dumbass which Eric had no trouble buying.

"Idiot kid," my uncle muttered, walking away. From down the hall, he called out, "Aw, sorry. Not you. Duncan."

The green Karmann Ghia was located by the police within a week. He'd abandoned the car, a note on the driver's seat, in the parking lot of an observation area on the north side of the Golden Gate Bridge.

The suicide, the note Duncan had written to his family, none of it directed attention to my uncle and Reckless John Rider's use-them-and-lose-them operation. With the suicide, Eric's mood lightened, an item off his Rider plate.

Eric did think it was well past time for me to return home. One problem with that? "I tossed my Ameripass my first night in the city," I said sheepishly. "My plan was to stay here."

That didn't fit Eric's plans. He bought me an airline ticket. I flew out of San Francisco International, arriving home for school with time to spare.

Flying over America, back to the Midwest, I looked down through the breaks in the clouds at the interstates, the traffic, when I could make it out, rolling predominantly to the west. Yet some, no, many rolled to all points east. And that made

me think of Duncan. I wondered where he was, rolling away
on a Greyhound bus.

I shit you not.

Verstehen sie?

Deep Cuts at the Inner Groove

Strom was thinking of the Bowie album, but not the single. He wouldn't touch those lyrics.

A summer weekday at the Inner Groove, set in the curve of the boomerang mall. Quiet at the record store after the stutter of the staplegun. He'd spent an hour posting Patti Smith LP sleeves helter-skelter over the bin of the poet-rocker's albums, sale priced with PSG rolling into town for a concert. Strom slapped a yellow legal pad down on the glass-topped case next to the cash register—under the glass, an assortment of tape head and record cleaners, incense burners, rolling papers, and pipes. *For Tobacco Products Only* on cardstock. Strom's degree was in English, American Lit, class of '78; now he used a legal pad to write pop song parodies, the latest a tweak on a Simon and Garfunkel song: "The Only Living Boy in Madison."

The past year, post-grad, he spent scuffling from one minimum wage job to another. To his parents, he was a contrarian. He dug the song "Misunderstood" from Pete Townshend and Ronnie Lane's *Rough Mix*; it had been his theme song, no apologies, to the age of twenty-three. Goddammit, it fit: he'd never planned on being out of school, that BA stuffed in his back pocket, forget a teaching certificate. Being misunderstood. Strom sent the leisure suit guys from HQ around the bend when he made an obscure, he thought, British folkie's LP—it was Ralph McTell—a number one in-store hit. Misunderstood—until he no longer wanted to be.

There had been a summerlong flirtation to no end. The irregular pop in by a pre-med student, never buying, who called herself Chatty Cathy. The white cross she'd pass along for free. Then she picked up with a former boyfriend. Strom was sorry to hear that. People moved on in their lives. He apparently didn't.

Before diving into another verse, he did an owl-head spin of the store. One customer, a woman killing midday time, flipped titles in the cassette tape gallery, row after row of plastic cases locked in by vertical rods. She click-clacked down the gallery, riffling through a twenty-foot wide, plastic-paged book.

Strom snagged the tape key, would've preferred lunch, but the manager—dubbed Frampton Plant because he considered himself the alchemized son of Peter Frampton and Robert Plant—was out with the leisure suits.

He walked over with the key, maybe the woman found a cassette that interested her. A man walked in: dress pants, blazer with a name badge on the lapel—an area bank—white shirt, tie. Call him a teller manager.

The woman glanced at Strom, shook him off.

The newcomer in business dress gave off a prickly vibe. Strom was in jeans and a wrinkled Inner Groove t-shirt. *I'm cool* nods as they passed each other. The newcomer continued to the cassettes.

Spot-checking the LP bins—errant asses slipped Foreigner into the Dan Fogelberg bin, Rolling Stones with Roxy Music, Beatles *with* the Stones—Strom lifted an eye. The teller manager dropped to his hands and knees and was peeking up the woman's cotton shift. She continued slowly through the plastic pages. Click. Clack.

"What the fuck—"

The peeper, unrushed, looked back, got to his feet, brushed off his knees, and walked out, just as Frampton Plant returned.

"Did you see that?" Strom asked.

Frampton Plant strutted behind the counter. After an "Immigrant Song" wail, he replied, "No, man. I just got back. What?"

* * *

A week later, Strom picked up lunch from the Golden Inn, the restaurant at the end of the mall. Walking in the drool-inducing sesame chicken and egg roll wave, he bopped down the mall to the store, the heavier elements of Neil Young and Crazy Horse's latest reverbing through his skull.

Thinking lunch, Neil's "Powderfinger" exploding in his head, it took Strom by surprise, seeing her emerge from the Your Hair Designed Salon, pulling straight ahead of him. The cassette browser. He considered stepping up along-side her, apologizing for what happened, but then again, she might not have been aware. She'd left after the peeper, didn't buy anything. He let it go, following her back to the record store.

Frampton Plant split as soon as Strom arrived. "Lunch date. Hold down the fort, man." A nod, a wink, he was gone. The woman was back in the gallery.

He was dipping the egg roll in a small plastic cup of Chinese hot mustard when the teller manager walked in. Strom checked the mustard-daubed appetizer halfway to his mouth. Like old times, the teller manager, glancing back at Strom, dropped to his hands and knees behind the woman. And he peeped.

Strom dropped the egg roll and charged down the gallery. He'd never in his twenty-three years been in a fight. The peeper bounced up, laughing, and dumped him into the cassettes. Click. Clack. The peeper walked away, unhurried.

The controlled rasp of the woman's glance couldn't spill Strom's mouthful of apologies. She shifted her purse strap, moved past him, and was gone.

He decided: get her safely to her car. At least give her a fistful of Inner Groove coupons. Strom could be a hero.

He slid the glass-paneled doors shut, locked the store up tight. Shrugging at three teens with money to burn and what-the-fuck attitudes, he said, "Be back. Emergency." He made for the parking lot.

The sun was high over the mall. Heatwaves curled serpentine from the blacktop and baking cars. He scanned the lot with an Eastwood squint.

There they were, less than a block away.

The peeper, the woman, embracing by a Firebird, its doors open, AC likely blasting. They were kissing.

"Fuck."

He walked back into the mall.

Not a hero. Not even for a day.

Like a Strange Old American Folk Song

She began writing to Peabody after his conviction that winter for attempted armed robbery. The jury went outside and stood in the slush of the parking lot for a collective cigarette and then was back in the box. That was how long it seemed to take. The jury foreman said, "Guilty," and Judge Harold M. Peterson handed twenty-year-old Peabody twenty to forty.

She began writing the day he was walked from the county jail to the state-owned white van with the crosshatched wire windows, his wrists cuffed and chained to his hobbled ankles.

She began writing to him as the white van drove across central Wisconsin, the winter landscape purgatorial, to the state correctional facility at Waupun.

She began writing as she thought a former classmate would, offering encouragement to someone she had graduated from high school with two years before. Without understanding it herself, the letter writing was her expiation.

She began writing because she remembered him so well from Pokegama Junction High School. Did he remember her when he met her that night last summer at Donny's Gas and Liquor Mart off Highway 8?

She began writing that she regretted having told him that night last summer that she remembered him so well. It was a weakness, that heart on her sleeve.

It threw him off his game, his plan fell apart, when this stocky, sandy-haired girl, Joy, Peabody didn't remember her name if he'd ever known it all, said, "I know you. You're Vince Peabody. Take that mask off. No one wears a ski mask in July, silly." She gave a horsey laugh. "Take it off." And as Peabody pulled the ski mask from his head, the tangle of sweat-soaked hair flattened to the curve of his skull, she picked up the telephone.

"I was just joking around." He pulled his hand from his jacket pocket. "See? I don't even have a gun. I don't own a pistol." Peabody still did not recognize her.

"Hi? This is Joy at Donny's, out on 8? I've got Vince Peabody here at the checkout counter and he just tried to rob us. Uh-huh. Yeah, I'll keep him here."

She began writing, It must have been unreal to you, meeting me at that time and place, two years after high school, everyone having gone their own way, college or tech school or remaining in town, working like me or drifting like you.

Peabody remembered her at the trial, the short, homely girl from high school, always on her own and watching him. He had blown her off. He had trouble enough skittering through that teenage arcade. Now here she was, testifying against him, still more of an outsider than he would ever be.

There was never any doubt that his conviction would hinge on her testimony. Peabody's toweringly ursine attorney from Duluth, Charles Schwindeman, could not shake her from the details of that night last summer.

"No, Mr. Schwindeman, he wasn't joking. He *said* he was joking when he found out that I knew who he was. But, no, there was no way he was joking."

His initial efforts to respond to her from the Waupun Correctional Institution caromed off his parietal, occipital and frontal bones in no fixed rhythm as he exercised in the prison yard, but those words, they remained in his head. He wanted whatever he finally sent to her to be polished, each word like an agate churned from the largest freshwater lake in the world, beautiful, cold and hard, and layered to a depth she could not fathom.

When Peabody put words to paper, he told her that if she felt bad, she shouldn't. This was all for the best, giving him time to think, to re-evaluate. In his cell, in the prison yard, in the cafeteria, in the prison laundry, Peabody evaluates and re-evaluates the many simple facets of the first twenty years of his life spent in Pokegama Junction. It eats him up.

She writes back, he responds, the call and response as from a strange old, half-forgotten American folk song that grows in her imagination to a crescendo until he asks for her hand. And Joy accepts his proposal.

He writes to her. She reads the words, I ache for the time when we can truly be together, and she believes in each and every one of them.

Counterweight

Danny Sizemore knew what he didn't like about Slim Nordquist: Slim looked like Curly, that skin-headed fat fuck from the Three Stooges, those gluttons for pain his old man loved to watch commit general mayhem at seventeen minutes a shot, all in the name of laughs. Thing was, Slim wasn't committed to laughs. When Slim went Stoogesque, he would mimic Curly's 1930s New Yorkese. "Am I gonna hoit ya? Why soitenly!" Clipping an overreaching knob in the back of the head, he would gurgle, "It's moida!"

Danny first met Slim when the fat man came up from the Twin Cities looking for Rusty H, Danny's predecessor in what they called, oddly prim, Sales and Marketing. Slim stopped by the house in the west end and asked his questions in a professional manner, none of the funny banter. Rusty needed to be hurt. Danny said he might be found in Two Harbors, West Duluth, Superior's North End. Nowadays, given any direction, finding Rusty H would be a losing proposition. For anyone.

Breakfasting at the Harmony Café, Danny got the news from Ducky Barnes. Slim was making a return trip to Duluth. He had someone to see.

Danny executed a double take worthy of Oliver Hardy, another of the old man's late show favorites. "Who?"

"Ooh, wise owl," chuckled the Ducks. He was a past and future yardbird of the Stillwater correctional facility, happy that he wasn't in line for the Slim Treatment. "It's you. Daniel X. Sizemore."

It was a Saturday in June. The sun was out. The ice was off Lake Superior. Tourists were in Canal Park. All these things were true, yet June had flipped to February.

Ducky split. Danny popped one of the pills from detox.

* * *

They said their goodbyes at Duluth International. The old man trundled his little green tank of life, the yellowed tubing a rubber mustache beneath the nose, his sugar babe Marla, twenty years his junior, had the carry-on over her shoulder stuffed with magazines and Dramamine, and Danny, the benefactor of the couple's Hawaii adventure.

"I don't know how you swung it, but thank you kindly." The old man clapped a hand on his shoulder. Marla, already bowled over by an attack of pre-flight nausea, smiled her thanks. Neither of them knew what Danny did for a living these days. All he ever told them was that it involved promotions in the Twin Ports with occasional visits to corporate in Minneapolis. Going into any more detail than that, Danny joked, he would have to kill them. Or they would die of boredom.

"Let me worry about that. I'm just happy I can do it."

Danny hadn't worried. Once he made the decision, he was all in. After cutting the smack, he sold the surplus. Dicier shit? Sure, but there was a clientele. His employer's customers were not siphoned off to the adulterated product. Minneapolis got its money. Danny got a little extra for himself and enough to send the old man and Marla on an all-expenses-paid vacation. He hadn't worried about it, hadn't overreached. Not too far.

He walked back to the short-term parking lot, heard the propulsive surge of jet engines. They were gone for two weeks. He knew he'd done right. No question. His father deserved one kick-ass vacation in his hard life and, since his time was short, there was no better time than now.

* * *

Danny arrived at this line of work after his layoff from the steel plant in that little shithole of a town up the North Shore. He'd commuted for nineteen years, wicked winters included. Then it was done. A friend living across St. Louis Bay in Superior, working for the railroad in between treatments for heroin addiction, turned him on to selling.

It was a difficult sell. At first mention, he walked out, shaking his head, wondering why in the hell life at the head of the lakes was such a shitcanned affair.

With the UI drying up, Danny indulged in one last wasted night on his own drug of choice. The evening went very bad very early because he got stupid with grief: the job loss, his girlfriend moving up the hill to her folks' place in Hermantown. Stinko on Jack, he sat in the backyard and dialed up everybody who had ever wronged him or done right by him, scorning in the one instance and thanking the others by singing theme songs from happy sitcoms of the Seventies and Eighties. It was awful for the scorned and the loved. His old man and Marla, on the "You're Beautiful List," had him packed away to detox before first light.

Discharged from detox with a clorazepate prescription, Danny called his friend. He was interested and, long story short, got himself a new job. Shortly thereafter, Rusty H got his layoff notice.

* * *

Clorazepate? No effect. Once home, he paced, popping his head out the front door to check the porch, peeking out the living room drapes. The view from the dining room window of the narrow walk between his place and the neighbor's. He looked from the kitchen window at the backyard, the daylilies, the garage, but knew he'd never spot him coming down the alley. Cup of instant coffee, up the stairs, looking out the front and back bedroom windows. Slim would know where to find him. Danny had played it straight except for the past few months. When Slim was looking for Rusty H, who did he ask for directions? Danny. Where? At the house Danny was pacing in.

He drummed the side of his head. He had to turn down the panic knob. Take another pill and breathe. He looked from the front bedroom window. It was what he needed. Lake Superior, Park Point, the Aerial Lift Bridge, Canal Park. Normalcy. Tourists crawling from shop to gallery to restaurant to ship canal and the lift bridge.

* * *

The vacationers were still a luau or two away from returning to their house on Greysolon, empty except for Danny on a step ladder in the attached garage, reaching blind in the dark space of the rafters. His hand touched two plastic-wrapped packages. The one on the left. The good stuff. Safe. The package to the right. The not-so-good. Danny pulled the bundle down and stowed it in his backpack.

* * *

Canal Park was a carnival without rides. Tourists hit chichi restaurants and shops and slept at the lakeside hotels. A strip joint grandfathered in with redevelopment received less than furtive looks from dads in cargo shorts. When Danny was a kid, all there had been between the ship canal and the warehouses was a burger-and-fries drive-in and a statue of Neptune. And the Aerial Lift Bridge over the canal. That was the constant. Canal Park would be preferable to waiting at home.

* * *

He split from the manic stroll of the out-of-towners and entered the deli-saloon near the bridge. A sailboat was leaving the marina. The bridge horn blared and the lift span began to rise so the vessel could pass through to the lake. He drank coffee, ate free popcorn, and watched the slow upward movement of the span and the downward grind of the solid block counterweights that lifted it from either end of the bridge.

* * *

Sunday morning, he watched from a Canal Park Drive bench. The crowds were slow to build, but when they did he was disappointed. He'd enjoyed the sounds of the lake, the gulls, the chirr of the early morning traffic.

He thought he might be better off walking the loop of the drive. Danny lifted the backpack and glanced across a break in the tourist stream. Slim was sitting on the bench opposite, lifted a hand, waggled his fingers, a Curlyesque greeting, temblors shaking his body. Then he flicked his hand around and gestured. Come here.

Danny's eyes narrowed. He launched himself off the bench. He walked at a near run, glancing back to see Slim cut gracefully through the tourists.

Traffic was at a standstill on Lake Avenue. The bridge gate was coming down. Both ran onto the lift span as the horn blew, long short long short. The deck was going to rise. Danny stopped and looked toward the harbor. A sailboat leaving port.

Slim stopped, shook his head. "That horn was pretty unnoivin'. Wait right there. It's as good a place as any." He pulled a .38. "You think you're the funny man?"

The bridge control house was a level up. The tender came out. "You can't be on the bridge. Get your butts off. Now!"

Slim swung the muzzle to the tender. "Get back to runnin' your bridge, Edmund Fitzgerald. This don't consoin you."

The tender looked at the gun, at Slim, at Danny, then back at the .38.

"Unless you *want* it to consoin you. Hey! I'm open to all comers."

The man shook his head and backed away to the bridge control house.

Slim rolled his eyes, shrugged his shoulders. "I'll have to kill him later anyways." The span began to move and he lurched and grabbed hold of the railing. "Cripes, youse nearly lucked out there."

The span rose. Danny watched the counterweight come down. He swung the backpack to his feet. "I've got what you want. I'm going to give it to you. We'll be good. Right? You go your way? I'll go mine?"

"Of course. We'll give you a gold watch." The counterweight ground down, the deck rose. Slim wagged the gun at the backpack. "In there?"

Danny nodded. Slim gestured for him to pass it over. Danny swung it past and Slim lunged as the backpack went over the end of the span. Down on his hands and knees, Slim watched as it dropped into the canal. The counterweight came from above and pressed him between its concrete mass and the span's steel edge with the irrevocable consequence of a boot stepping on a June bug.

It takes three minutes to lower the counterweights and raise the bridge span. It took three minutes, even with the counterweight crushing down on Slim's head and shoulders. The tender stepped from the control house. He and Danny looked at each other.

The sailboat passed below, out to the blue, wide-open lake.

At the Head of the Lakes

The night, with its streetlights and traffic lights, the tavern neon and bar signs advertising Northern Premium Beer and other vanished brews, was kinder to downtown Superior than daylight. Morning featured a taint throughout the city: a paucity of trees other than winter-hardy conifers; low, empty storefronts with FOR LEASE signs in dusty display windows; a downtown stricken more than thirty years before by the building of a mall that never seemed to take root; the booming commerce of ninety-seven bars in a community of approximately twenty-six thousand-odd denizens. There was the constant coin toss. Heads, it will be wet and cold, or tails, it will be dry and cold under a heavy slate-gray sky. When the coin stood stock-still on its grooved rim, it could mean the hard times would get worse. It was as if the city, in its distant past promoted by developers as the next Chicago, had slipped its moorings and drifted now, minus captain and crew, on the waters of Lake Superior. Nights were kinder.

After a week in May of wind and rain off the still ice-covered Lake Superior, what Steven Piper with his graphic artist's eye called The Week of Black Umbrellas, the storm tailed off to the west, across St. Louis Bay, and up and over the hills of Superior's neighbor, Duluth. Spring, however brief it might end up being, had arrived on a southerly breeze, the sidewalks and streets wet and steaming with humidity. Piper cracked open the windows of his apartment and graphic arts studio situated above Broadway and Hammond and breathed deeply of the tardy season. He was thirsty and it was time to get out.

A freelancer, Piper preferred the dismal weather—the rain, the snow, the cold—that funneled into the head of the Great Lakes because it kept him indoors, focused and at the work he contracted for with agencies and publishers in Milwaukee, Minneapolis-St. Paul, and Chicago, as well as that brought in by his recent expansion beyond the Third Coast. When the weather moderated and the day-glo green buds exploded in the rare deciduous tree, when there was no cold blow off the lake, he was ready to abandon his PC and Wacom Intuos4 tablet in the studio, he was ready to seek out his version of rejuvenation in the taprooms and dives of Superior.

He slipped on a pair of old paint-splotched Florsheim loafers, an affectation because he did not paint at all, and headed out that afternoon, waving at Ed Diaz as he passed through the building's lobby, the baker standing in the doorway of his shop. Diaz rolled his eyes. "Uh-oh, lock up the good booze."

Piper juggled his keys, flipped them over his shoulder, danced back to catch them.

Ed shook his head and laughed. "Get out of here, *pendejo*."

Piper's eyes twinkled with a shine like any other insincere boozer's, but what could Diaz do? He followed Piper to the arched entry of the Romanesque building. "Say, man, you want me to pick you up somewhere later and bring you back to your place?" The baker was like a spinster aunt. "Leave me your keys, then you won't be driving around hurting yourself or anybody else. What do you say, just walk yourself downtown?"

Piper couldn't help toying with Diaz. He'd recognized that the old queen had an unreserved horn for him the day he moved into the building. The attraction was unrequited, but useful when Piper was short on cash. He flashed the older man his bad boy pout. "If you wake up at four and figure I'm not back at my place, you know where to find my spare. I'll park the car down by the BN yards." Piper laughed.

Diaz nodded, his cheeks and forehead torched with blush. He grumbled *pendejo* one last time. He just wanted to take care of Piper, watch over him.

Piper drove his decades old Datsun, a faded butterscotch shoebox with a cassette player and nonfunctional AM/FM radio, six blocks to an unpaved, toxic lot along the rail yard west of Tower Avenue and sat there with his windows rolled down. Even this dumping ground smelled of spring, he thought. His thirst quickening, he left the Datsun and began to walk south on the avenue's battered, weed-fringed sidewalk.

The Basement was Piper's tavern of choice, but that didn't stop him from turning in at a quiet topless joint, the small stage with its brass pole dark in the afternoon. He had a quick shot with Schmitty the bartender, who ended her own exotic dancing career over seventeen years earlier at the Star Lite Lanes. Bowling and boobs. Piper befriended her at the Star Lite when he celebrated his eighteenth birthday. Next up was the Party on the Point Night Club, formerly an upscale men's clothing store, where Cheek impatiently waited for that night's band from Cloquet to show and set up. They had a double together and Piper encouraged him to lighten up, it was still early.

He stopped at each bar on the west side of Tower Avenue, pounding back drink after drink, greeting his familiars after the long working hibernation in the studio. Before he reached The Basement's front door he was slipping into that recognizable and, to him, pleasant brownout state.

The Basement wasn't in a basement, no steps in or out or anywhere else on the premises because of liability issues. The tavern was owned and tended by Hoover, a former English major who presided over the bar like a bookseller, attracting local academics, English professors and lecturers, the university theatre crowd for a little drama and added comedy, and Art Department folk.

The woman Piper saw at the bar couldn't be categorized as one of the regulars. She was in her forties and elfin and could have easily passed for thirty-five years, Piper's age, or younger. And she was sitting on the barstool next to his customary perch. He nodded and, as he sat down, said, "Good evening."

Piper ordered a double. The woman looked at him, once, twice, three times, as he ordered another. He turned and smiled. "Excuse me, am I invading your personal space?"

She ignored him and nursed her pint of India Pale Ale. "You should really try this microbrew, it's, h'm, let's see if they have it here. Hoover," he called, "Do you carry something called Hellcat IPA?"

Hoover ignored him, having recent experience with the woman. She did, however, respond to Piper. "I can believe you've had plenty of experience with hellcats." Her voice was so gravel-bound Piper supposed she copped her first butt from her mother's ashtray the day she learned to walk. He heard a blend of Lauren Bacall, Suzanne Pleshette, and Brenda Vaccaro and in his bemusement thought the voice sexy rather than snappish and he was charmed. He bought the next round, believing he was on the way to charming her back.

There had been clear skips in the record. He noticed these like bits of side conversation, a word or two that would prick up his ears. Then the brownout shutter would come down again. For how long? He couldn't have said. For all he knew, it was happening outside of himself rather than in his own head.

She must have introduced herself at some point and he must have introduced himself as well. She knew his name and he liked how her rough voice said, "Piper." Not Steven. Piper. And then she would laugh and he would join her. But then, the blank again.

They had moved to a table, who knew when, the woman and Piper. She was going through a divorce. If he had been sober he would have excused himself and disappeared out The Basement's backdoor, into the alley, to his car in the parking lot. If he had parked nearby. He knew he hadn't parked nearby. So why would he slide his keys across the table to her. What was her name? She knew he was Piper. He slid the Datsun's keys across the table. She laughed, a high, crystalline laugh for someone with such a low, smoky voice. She laughed, smoke and glass, and he was gone again.

The woman was crying. The last time he'd seen her she'd been laughing. What was with the sadness? Then, back to the brownout.

She was into a story, the story of how her husband broke it to her. Her husband invited her to go for a ride. He had something to show her. She went willingly. Their marriage had been rocky for a year or two, but in the last few weeks they had come to an unspoken, she assumed, understanding, some temporary armistice—no more yelling, no more tears from her or their two teenage daughters. There was a calm, she said, no more arguments over inane bullshit. She went along for the ride. "I was like a dog, a pet dog, you know. Happy to go for a ride with the master.

"We drove south out of Superior on old 35, through South Superior, past Greenwood Cemetery, beyond Pattison State Park. The windows were rolled down. The radio was tuned to a rock and roll station in Duluth. If I could have just captured that moment. It was the best our marriage had been in years."

South of the state park, her husband had taken a right. A quarter mile into the woods.

Piper's reception fluttered and faded. Then back again.

"There was this small cabin-like place, cheaply built and ugly with faded purple siding. The ground was covered with pine needles. He parked and we both just stared out the windshield at this cabin. It didn't look like anyone had lived there in years, you know. Probably full of mice."

She had glanced at her husband and was surprised to see him looking at her. "What?" she asked.

"I've signed a six-month lease and I move in this week, Jill." Piper caught that. Her name had to be Jill. "I have to get my head together. I can do it out here."

"Then," she told Piper, "I really felt like the pet dog taken for a ride. I was the happy pet dog that didn't have a clue she was being taken to the vet's to be put down."

Jill. That was her name, he remembered that.

Jill was yelling at him, her voice a lamp switched on, brightening the dark corners of his consciousness. "I can't believe you just asked me that." What? "I tell you the horrible end to my sucky marriage and you essentially—essentially, right?—basically, *basically* ask if I want to get laid. I can't believe that." He still liked her voice.

The last time he saw her—Jill, he knew the name from her long end-of-marriage story—the last time he saw Jill in

The Basement, she was back on the stool at the bar. Where he had first seen her.

Piper began walking home on Tower Avenue, heading north. The wind was off the lake. Who cared when that happened. You lived in Superior, you expected the wind to shift and penetrate your core. His brownouts occurred a block at a time, in between the streetlights on each corner. At one point he thought he saw Jill walking ahead of him, under another streetlight and alone. He peeled away, down Eleventh Street. He didn't want her to think that he was following her.

Sunday afternoon and each window in his apartment was an erasure smudged page. "It's a metaphor for graphic artist's block," he once quipped, though typically, for him, it signified the onset of a creative burst. This Sunday afternoon there was nothing more than the series of blank pages.

His sinuses were clogged. Piper could never seem to blow his nose enough after a night out. No hangovers, only the sleeping in and the stuffed nose. He rolled upright at the edge of his bed and reached for something, a tissue, a used handkerchief, a sock. Anything would do at this point. He was still dressed, but was pleased to see that at least he had taken off his loafers.

He decided to shower before going down to Ed Diaz's bakery for coffee and a couple of Ed's heavy cake doughnuts. As the hot spray from the shower head exfoliated his face and ran down his body, the previous evening came back, though difficult to read, like an unsuccessful print job. The Basement. The woman named Jill. Had he given her his car keys? He would have to check his pockets.

There was the walk home, what he remembered of it. She had been up ahead of him, her cute hind end. Others had been out on the street, out past closing time. Had he driven out to the Point, the sandy strip of land abutting the lake? Not in the state he'd been in. No. But why did he recall headlights passing under the trees? The tree limbs that overhung a stretch of Wisconsin Point Road?

Toweling himself off, he went and checked the pockets of the pants he had worn the night before. A mix of spare change and crumpled bills, but no keys. "Damn." That settled it. After the doughnut brunch at Diaz's bakery he would go back downtown and start tracking down the woman named Jill. "What the hell'd I give her my keys for?" At least she wouldn't have known where to find the Datsun. Unless he had drawn her a map.

Piper dressed, slipped on his Florsheim's, and immediately felt grit in both shoes. He took the loafers off and turned one over, then the other. Sand poured out from both.

Diaz's bakery attracted the neighborhood's artsy, beat element and college students, as well as older folks making a Sunday muffin run, something to breakfast on and share with the dog while reading the newspaper. When Piper walked in most of the tables were taken over by students with MacBooks and laptops, not one of them talking, just tapping the keys of their machines and focusing on the monitors. Diaz, waiting on a customer, nodded at him. He took a table by a window looking out on Hammond Avenue and a convenience store.

Diaz left his niece Luz to work the counter and brought Piper his usual. "Afternoon, man." Outside, the sky had turned a uniform gray and a wind out of the north blew a sheet of newsprint down the avenue. "Things back to normal, eh," the baker said, shaking his head.

"Meaning?"

"The weather. You know, man. It's Superior."

Piper sipped the coffee, dunked his doughnut, took a bite and glanced around. "Do you know if my car's in the lot today?"

Diaz looked back at Luz wiping down the glass counter. Two tables had emptied, the keying chirr diminished, notebooks snapped shut. His fingertips toyed with the porcelain container of sugar, Sweet'N Low, and Splenda packets. "Sure. Any reason it shouldn't be?"

Relieved, Piper nodded his head. "Well, yes. I thought I gave my car keys to a woman I met last night at The Basement. I'd been thinking to myself that I'd slid them across the table to her." He rolled his eyes. "The latest edition of Piper's Toasted Times."

Ed shifted his chair back and away from the table. "Say, Luz, why don't you take off."

"I still have some clean up to do in the back, Uncle Ed."

"That's okay. I'll take care of it."

"If you're sure," she said, as he walked her to the door.

"Come on. You folks, too," he said to the last full table. Piper moved to leave, but Diaz waved for him to stay.

After locking the bakery door, he came back and sat across from Piper. It began raining, the nickel- and dime-size drops smacking against the nearest windows. "Listen, you did give her your car keys."

Piper slumped back. "Aw."

"It was getting late and I called up to your place. There was no answer, so I headed out looking for your loopy ass. I found this little woman in the BN lot, screwing with your car door in the dark. She must've thought that I was going to assault her. She pulled out a, I don't know, a knife, I thought. We got into it, man, and I hit her. I've never hit a woman in my life. But I thought she was jacking your car, and she came at me with a knife. When I hit her, I hit her hard.

"She went down. Your keys went flying. The knife—that was really pepper spray."

Piper leaned forward and shook his head.

"I thought I'd just knocked her out. But it was worse. She was dead.

"I put her in the trunk. Then I found you—*finally*—wandering a couple blocks away. We took the body out to the Point, to the Superior Entry." Diaz's voice took on a more spirited tone. "Someone had to watch out for the Holy Artist, man. You need a bodyguard, a guard from yourself on days like yesterday."

"What did you do at the ship entry, Ed?"

"Get this, there was a map drawn onto a bar napkin showing her where the car was. You draw pretty well even when you're totally wasted, man."

"The entry, Ed. What happened out there?"

"I tossed her body in, man. Into the lake." A smile flared across his face. "I did it for you."

Barman

Freddie Everett didn't blame his daughter one bit for the way she felt at times. His grandson had been shifty since... when? Freddie counted the boy's years, rolled them between his fingertips and thumb like his tiny blood pressure pills on a string, a rosary for the heart. Yes, twelve. Since Josh turned twelve, he had been a recalcitrant little punk. Carmen, when Josh's behavior was off the goddammed charts, blamed the kid for her *clinical* depression. Whatever the hell clinical depression was. Freddie didn't know, never heard of it in his eighty-eight years until Carmen's diagnosis came at her long distance, a letter, and a follow-up phone call from the Duluth clinic. That was a good hour's drive away. Now Freddie Everett's grandson was twenty and in jail, arrested for attempting to rob a drugstore. He didn't like calling him a punk, even in his head, but goddammit all. The kid wanted some drug. OxySomething. And now Carmen was down in the dumps. Freddie thought he would cheer her up, if only for a little while. He'd paid a surprise visit to Josh at the county lockup the night before and had a good talk with the kid. This morning, he'd decided to drop in and give Carmen the lowdown.

It was a straight shot, fourteen miles from Port Nicollet, south on 33 to her place in Pokegema Junction. The drive cut through wonderfully dense woods, past the occasional, and rare nowadays, mom-and-pop dairy farm. Carmen and Josh lived in a yellow and brown-sided two-bedroom rambler built in the fifties, the yellow and brown asbestos-cement siding faded like an old photograph. Freddie had bought the house for them when Josh was a baby. It was tucked into little more than a turnaround off the state highway, kicked up against a dark wall of white pine, tamarack, and black spruce.

Fourteen miles. Time enough to ponder. It had been difficult to tell Josh his story precisely because Freddie Everett was not a braggart; he couldn't tolerate windbags. He'd only told one other person. Years ago. That was hard enough and it was only because Jimmy Grochowski, to a limited extent, had been involved. But he told his grandson the story, and, thick as he could play it at times, Josh got the point. Sometimes, at a particular age, you need someone to lay it out for you, give you the options.

A Port Nicollet municipal judge gave Freddie the options all the way back in 1939. Options when he needed them.

"Your sister is offering you a hundred dollars to get a new start in Minneapolis. That's an incredible gift, Fred." The judge watched him, thinking he would jump at the money and the big city. There was nothing. The judge cleared his throat. "I can offer you two other choices. Join the army—I believe you could learn from such an experience. Or I could follow the letter of the law and sentence you to a year in the Gordon work camp. You could learn from that experience as well, but not in any useful way to you or the public."

The clock tick in the judge's chambers was like a door tapping against its frame, lightly, over and over again. Freddie never considered accepting his sister's hundred-dollar stake. The work camp? Prison? No.

The judge raised an eyebrow.

"I'll enlist, sir."

After a twenty-year hitch that included the European and Pacific theaters of World War II, and then the Korean War, he returned to Port Nicollet, on the south shore of Lake Superior, and never left the area again. He settled into what he had learned in the army's quartermaster school and, later, through the management of an enlisted men's club in postwar Bavaria. In Port Nicollet, he managed the Blue Grotto.

On an early spring day in 1965, it was Freddie's turn to offer options.

That day began for him like any other. He dressed for work in the crisply laundered white shirt with French cuffs, the razor-creased black trousers, and the burgundy vest with the Blue Grotto logo. The Windsor-knotted necktie, perfect. A pair of black Ferragamo loafers. He donned his camel overcoat and went out for a Lucky Strike while he waited for the cab on 5th Street.

He measured out the coming day with each draw on the unfiltered cigarette: brew a pot of coffee behind the bar, do a once- and twice-over, ensure everything was fit for the day's operation. At closing time, he'd leave a couple of bucks extra for the Wickstrom girl, Betty, who swabbed the Blue Grotto early each morning. She was a nice kid from Port Nicollet's North End, the neighborhood he'd grown up in, returned to after the wars. The Blue Grotto. Freddie Everett treated the Blue Grotto as if it were his own.

Driving to Pokegema Junction, he recalled the day in 1965 when it had been the time in-between. It happened each weekday. He sipped coffee from the quartermaster mug that travelled with him from Bavaria. The martini lunch crowd, that group of Port Nicollet civic boosters, the lords and ladies of city government, had been and gone. The TV burbled images, Art Fleming hosting *Jeopardy!*, the sound off, Freddie answering correctly with a question. It was that time before the afternoon crowd arrived: the regulars pushing open the door, together, solo, with looks like, "How the hell did I get here," "You again," and the Jackie Gleason catchphrase, "And awaaay we go!" But that day, the time in-between changed.

A sweaty muggins of a punk broke the routine. He was somewhere between the ages of indeterminate youth, twenty-one to infinity. At Fort Ord in 1939, he would have been a raw recruit like Freddie.

Vegetable beef soup left cold on the stove for days on end. Freddie got that drift from him. A meat stink. He didn't know why. Nothing against the soup, but the way the odor peeled off the kid in waves was like old BO. He'd thought, "Okay," and took one more sip of coffee before setting the heavy mug down on the bar top.

Exuding the soup funk, the kid also had a nervous sheen from brow to cheek that caught like a fever in the bar light. He wasted no time in showing why. The gun was a low caliber piece that could still kill a person. If he had a plan, it wasn't a good one. Freddie doubted he'd spent more time on his scheme than deciding on a rapid fire four or five steps: "I'll steal a gun. I'll rob a bar—The Blue Grotto. I'll commit to it at two thirty and be out by two forty-five, tops."

Freddie didn't lift the mug up, not another sip. The barrel of the gun twitched in the young man's juiced hand. Maybe he expected Freddie to tremble, eyes wide. It flummoxed the kid when the barman didn't respond. Instead, Freddie's hands lay flat on the bar top on either side of the mug.

The kid shrugged. "Okay, gramps." Freddie was forty-four at the time. "Dump the cash register drawer into this." An empty Wonder Bread bag, so cheering with the red, yellow, and blue balloons.

Freddie blinked once, not from fear, but to stop from making a dry-witted crack about the plastic bread bag. And then he reached up and placed the tip of his right index finger on the muzzle. He had always treated any place of employment as his own and, as he would say, you did not shit in Freddie Everett's place of employment. Anybody who knew him was aware of this. The would-be bandit found out sooner than most.

"What's your name?" Freddie asked.

The kid looked down at the older man's fingertip pressed against the muzzle.

"Come on. What's your name?"

He flicked his eyes back to Freddie's and blinked. Nonplussed. "George." George, and Freddie didn't doubt he'd given his real name, looked like he could kick himself a round trip to the Twin Cities and back.

"George? I'm Everett, Freddie Everett."

George nodded, then scrunched his eyes, the plan coming apart, and shook his head.

"Once, back when I was a young man, I was in a tight spot, probably a lot like the one you're in now. Squeezed, George. *Squeezed*. Brought up in front of a judge, I thought, 'This old so-and-so won't understand a thing.' But he did know something. He gave me three options. The one I picked, it worked out. We've all got them. If you'd let me, I'd like to tell you what I believe your options are—"

"Say—"

"Hear me out, hear me out. I'm not a judge, but let me lay out a few choices for you to consider. Do you have enough money for a one-way Greyhound ticket to Minneapolis?"

The kid's brow creased, adding it up. "I'm not sure. Maybe."

"Don't think too hard on it. We could call the depot, check the prices. If you're a bit short, I'll make up the difference. But here's the thing if you choose that option, George. You have to agree to get your ass out of town on the next available Minneapolis-bound bus."

The finger on the muzzle did not, would not waver.

"That's option one. The second option is, I walk you over to the U.S. Navy recruiting office and you enlist for four years. Any of the other branches would do, too, but I'm thinking, for you, the Navy."

The kid began to look like he was the luckiest person in Port Nicollet.

"Option three, probably not the best from your point of view, but here goes. A good friend and favorite customer of mine is coming through the front door, the one right behind you, in a few minutes. It's time for his afternoon coffee break. We shoot the shit, drink java, and watch a little bit of a soap opera. He's Officer Jimmy Grochowski, with the Port Nicollet PD. I have a feeling you're a relatively smart kid. I can see you weighing your options. Grochowski? Bear of a man. Not a good bet."

The upshot? Officer Grochowski, who protested and encouraged Freddie to press charges, drove George to the bus depot. Freddie helped the kid with cash for a one-way ticket and an additional stake for when he reached Minneapolis, as well as names, job connections.

Last night, after telling the story to Josh, his grandson asked, "Weren't you afraid he'd shoot?"

"Hell, no. I'd fought most of my adult life. Germany. Japan. Korea. I'd seen too much to be afraid for myself.

Besides, it was my damn bar. That kid George had no right."
It wasn't braggadocio, it really wasn't.

"You weren't afraid to die?"

Freddie shook his head. "Dying would've been nothing."

His grandson nodded. Josh got it. Freddie was sure he understood that he had options too. Before Freddie left, Josh put on that faint, wry smile of his. "You think it still works that way, Grandpa." Freddie hadn't thought of it until now, but that last from Josh, it wasn't a question.

A squad car driven by a county deputy, the deputies interchangeable, each with a thirteen-year-old's pimply face and the physique of Charles Atlas, was leaving as Freddie pulled in at Carmen's. He waved, but the deputy didn't wave back. Freddie shook off the snub. He was eager to see Carmen and tell her about his talk with Josh.

As Freddie parked, he noticed Carmen alone on the front stoop, her hand tight over her mouth. He swallowed. His hands dropped from the steering wheel.

She reached the car as Freddie, feeling his years, climbed out. "Goddammit. Goddammit, Dad. Josh hanged himself." His daughter sobbed then, a jagged, tearing sound.

It wasn't 1939.

It wasn't 1965.

In this late year of Freddie Everett's life, his grandson had found there was another option.

Boomer in the Sky with Toxics

The dog sat in the doorway watching Boomer work in the darkened bathroom. Rummaging in the medicine cabinet, penlight held between his teeth, searching out Andrew's meds, he turned and glanced at the dog, ran the light over him, a Shih Tzu-dachsie mix with a pronounced underbite. A hairy meatloaf. They fed him too much, couldn't help themselves. The light hit the dog's eyes, the one good one, the other sheathed in a milky cataract, and his tail drummed the floor.

Boomer took the penlight from his mouth, whispered, "Go away," then turned back to the cabinet with its regimented orange plastic containers. A pharmaceutical wonderland, the majority in his nephew Andrew's name, the rest belonging to Don and Joan, his brother and sister-in-law, pills to treat their late middle age: high cholesterol, high blood pressure, menopause, peeing too often or not enough, and boner pills. "Little brother." He popped one into his mouth.

But it was Andrew who really had the goods. Boomer couldn't wipe out the stash, the kid was battling AIDS, just a taste from each prescription, shake a few samples out into the plastic sandwich bags stuffed into the pockets of his field jacket. He counted out the caplets, the tabs, the gel caps, and, taking some, wondered what the horse pills would do.

At the distant rumble of the garage door, the dog waddled off with its welcome home bark and, in a rush now, Boomer made a mess of his drug dispensing, tablets ricochet-ticking in the bathroom sink. It wasn't a complete botch, he had time to pop a few more pills into his mouth, shove the baggies deeper into his jacket pockets, and glide off, agile for fifty-nine, the wet tracks he made coming in on the carpeted hallway encountered on the way out, down the stairs, past the Christmas tree and the presents that Don, Joan, and Andrew would be opening soon, now that they were home, and quietly, so quietly, Boomer slipped out the front door, the kitchen light popping on behind him, out into the cold and starry O Holy Night, willing himself to feel whatever he had ingested, Boomer in the sky with toxics.

Boomer, one hundred twenty pounds and dropping, had arrived in Port Nicollet just after midnight on the twenty-fifth of December. The bus beat its scheduled arrival time, so his son, Gary, wasn't at the depot to pick him up as planned. Boomer didn't see Saint Nick streaking across the sky either, although Keith Richards's cover of "Run Rudolph Run" rocked through his aural memory. Gary had wired him the money for the bus trip up from Tennessee, where South Shore Grain, Boomer's employer, had sent him for rehab. No one seemed to understand that he and rehab, although nodding acquaintances, had never shook hands and agreed on anything like the efficacy of treatment. He had stopped the smack, but that had been on his own. Shit was unheard of in Port Nick in the sixties. Things had changed.

Boomer drove Tom Dean's '41 Ford pickup truck along the snow-packed streets of Port Nick, away from Don and Joan's house. He and Tommy D, passing a doobie back and forth over the engine, had overhauled the truck back in the eighties. They took it when they went fishing in the Hayward Lakes area. Good times. Now, his wife in mind, he had an erection—the damn boner pill. His wife. Were they still married? They wed twenty-eight years ago. Beautiful Mama was what he called Diana. She'd laugh and call him Wasted Daddy. The laughter ended, long gone, he understood that. He couldn't show his face now, especially not with all the blood in his body concentrated in his groin. It would wear off like everything else.

He squatted at Tommy D's place in the Lakeshore neighborhood of Port Nicollet, not that Tommy D knew he was staying there. Boomer knew the ins-and-outs of Port Nick. Tommy D and his second family were Christmassing in Florida, far away from the south shore of Lake Superior. He guessed his old partner in crime wouldn't mind. Boomer had to land somewhere, temporarily, or at least feel like he could. He was hurtling toward the end of the year. There was that humming in his head over the past several days, an ache and a wave of sound building like the last chord of the Beatles' "A Day in the Life." He couldn't stand still, waiting out the crescendo, the peak and crash, so his plan was to keep on moving through the last week of December, either on foot or by using Dean's collector-plated pickup. And, of course, sleep sparingly at the Lakeshore house. That was his plan.

He woke up in a guestroom, not cool to occupy the master bedroom. It took a few heart-racing minutes to register that he was in the guestroom of somebody's home and not in a room at the treatment center. Tommy D's. That's right. Still, in bed, without moving a muscle, his body did wind sprints. He hyperventilated. Slow down. Slow down. There. He rolled his head in the direction of the bedside alarm clock and its red digits. Late afternoon of his first—second? third?—full day back in town. It was dark outside.

Boomer phoned Gary from Tommy D's basement rec room. The green felt surface of the pool table, the sound system's speakers pockmarking the ceiling, an eye-swallowing flat screen television, DVDs, compact discs, record albums. He called his son, who, with caller ID, immediately asked, "Tom?"

"No, this is Dad."

Boomer noted the unspoken letdown.

"Where'd you take off to the other night? That morning? Greta and I went to pick you up. You know what we saw? We saw the bus leaving for Duluth. Taillights heading west and the other passengers standing around, waiting for their rides, but not you. Did Tom pick you up?"

"I—yeah."

"Merry Christmas. That story's BS. I know the Deans left town for the holidays. Tell me you didn't break in."

"Merry Christmas to you, too. No, I did not 'break in.' What the hell. Tom gave me a key."

"Before you went to Tennessee for treatment? Dad?"

Boomer didn't respond.

"I'm going to come over and pick you up. You can bunk here. Greta's gone to her folks' place in the Cities till New Year's Eve."

"No, you don't have to do that. I was going to go over to my father's."

"Grandpa's pretty bad now. Worse, I should say. Mom irritates the hell out of him every time she stops in. She's just trying to help. Me? He doesn't even recognize me anymore. I tell him I'm Michael's son. He remembers Michael." Michael. Boomer pre-1968.

"Well, that's why I wanted to get back to Port Nicollet. Thanks for the scratch, by the way. He's the reason I wanted to get back. Take care of my father."

His son's biting laugh. "Dad, you can't even take care of yourself."

* * *

Earlier in the year, the docs diagnosed the old man with senile dementia. Boomer couldn't expect his kid brother and sister-in-law to be the caretakers, not with Andrew as sick as he was. Boomer drove over to his childhood home, the edge dulled by some weed of Tommy D's that he came across in a tea tin, a tumbler of Jack, and a pastel collection of Andrew's pills.

Someone had cleared the sidewalk, the shovel standing in a snow bank near the house. Boomer tried the front door. Locked. He could have predicted as much. The sky was clear and there was no wind, the temperature well below zero. His eyes watered, turning the Christmas lights of the neighborhood into a colorful scattering of bijouterie.

The old man shot off the tracks after Boomer's mother stroked out and died. All within a year. A quiet death in their bed on a Sunday morning. Boomer had dropped by that weekend after Thanksgiving, expecting to help her put up the light-festooned reindeer in the front yard. An ambulance beat him to the house.

He was about to leave after pounding on the door one last time, thinking maybe the old man was over at Uncle Ray's, but, glancing around the back, he saw the Pontiac. Boomer knocked again and jumped when he noticed the white-haired old man peering out through the sidelight.

How many days had he been in Tennessee? How many weeks? Looking at his father, he could have been in out-of-state treatment for years.

"Yes?"

"Hi, Dad." His father studied his face. "Can I come in? It's freezing out here."

"Michael?"

"Yeah."

Once inside, his father looked at him with a dreaming eye and said, "Well, my gosh. Michael. You're Michael. You're my son."

Boomer excused himself to use the bathroom. He took a slow, stuttering whiz and then ran the tap while he went through the medicine cabinet. Pills for his father's dementia? He had them, a lot of them, and he obviously wasn't taking them. Boomer swept the pill bottles up and deposited them into his jacket pocket.

He buzzed. The old man maundered, confused grievances, some final sense that his mind was no longer what it had been. "I went to Old Town and, did you know, some ruthless bastards tore down my mother's house. Tore it the hell down. It's a vacant lot and the city has been using it to dump snow from its street cleaning operation. I stopped in at Solberg's across the street and he had the balls to tell me the house came down years ago. I'm going to talk to a lawyer about it. This will not stand."

Boomer was lightheaded. This will not stand. His apolitical father quoting the first George Bush?

His father told him to come and look, he had something to show him in the spare bedroom. Boomer blinked and he was in that bedroom's open doorway. There were framed photographs laid out on the bed: his father with his brothers, Gus and Ray, kids of the Depression, posing in their Port Nicollet Old Town backyard, Uncle Gus's high school graduation portrait, Uncle Gus receiving a ribbon or a medal from General Mark Clark, all the brothers and sisters in Uncle Ray's living room for a group picture, must have been taken in the seventies. There were others, all with

Uncle Gus as the focus. The folded flag in its presentation frame. An Ike jacket from the Korean War.

"It's in honor of my twin. Gus. He died, you know." Yes, Boomer knew. Uncle Gus had kicked it three years ago.

He left his father's house and sat in the pickup, in some zone, shivering. The key was in the ignition, the heat was on full, the snow, white feathers really, had begun to fall. The payoff, sitting, waiting, was when the old man left the house. And Boomer followed as he drove off in the Pontiac.

His father drove slowly and Boomer got the impression, maybe mistaken, maybe not, that the old man was wary of the snow banked on either side of the Port Nicollet streets, mounded high at the corners, that the snow banks were encroaching on him. The thought made Boomer cautious.

North of downtown, his father pulled into the parking lot of the abandoned railroad depot and Boomer parked on the street, watching as the Pontiac slowly circled the low building. After the sixth or seventh circuit, Boomer pulled in and blocked the old man's progress. He walked up to the driver's side of the Pontiac, the car's high beams flashing, the horn blaring.

"Dad," he tapped on the window and his father rolled it down.

"Move your damn pickup!"

"Dad. It's me. Michael. What are you doing? What are you looking for?" The cold, the stolen drugs, the thieved liquor in his veins, he just wanted to curl up, maybe on one of those high snow banks, curl up and fall asleep. But he couldn't. He was hurtling, the chord had yet to peak, but when it did. A day in the life.

"There used to be a convenience store here."

Boomer glanced over his shoulder at the Port Nicollet depot sign that remained at the roofline, the depot windows boarded up in the last five years, *No Trespassing* signs posted. "No more. They moved. What did you want to pick up?"

The old man didn't have to think over his response. "One of those frozen beef-and-bean burritos I can throw in the microwave."

I want to curl up, Dad. "I can pick that up for you. Why don't you follow me back to the house and then I'll run over to Junior's Market and pick up a couple of those for you?"

His father thought this over, this old man who used to reach into the backseat for a blind swipe when young Boomer gave him lip. When he found the pot in Boomer's bedroom, making him box, box as if they were Ali and Frazier, going a few rounds in the narrow kitchen. His mom's yelling and crying. His father thought over Boomer's offer, his eyes blinked. Boomer wondered, Who are you? Then his father, the stranger, said, "Okay."

Okay. "Cool. Wait, say. See. I've already"—he dug in his jacket pocket—"I've already picked your prescription up for you, too. Let's see. It says, take two with a meal."

"Yeah?"

"Yeah. So take these with you. Follow me back to the house. I'll get you your burrito. Beef and bean with green chili, right?"

"Yeah."

* * *

A few days later, a nighttime drive in late December. Diana. Beautiful Mama. She'd kicked him to the curb, moved herself out to an apartment on Larch Avenue, close to downtown, closer to the main drag. Boomer drifted by the brick fourplex in the pickup. Drifted by like a love-wracked sixteen-year-old. How could it be that the love of a woman and a son were not enough? He had given Diana a number of excuses and once thought to add, but did not, "I guess I must not care." That would have been a lie, used only to encourage her to give up on him, finally. Which, of course, she did.

He drifted by, a full moon in December, and with the last pass scraped the sides of twelve snow-covered cars parked along Larch Avenue.

* * *

It may have been New Year's Eve when he came to, cramped and cold, on the floor of a camper trailer. Fingers and toes numb, he tried to place where he was and forced himself to his feet. Looking out the small window, he saw that it was Don's backyard. He was in his kid brother's winterized cracker box trailer.

And there was Don, Joan tagging along behind, charging out of the house, through the snow, headed for the trailer and Boomer.

The kid got in some good licks, the flailed Boomer pinballing around in the confined space, Don accusing him, in between the thrown punches and kicks, of trying to kill Andrew by stealing his medication. When she finally thought the beating had gone on long enough, Joan broke it up. "I'll call Gary to come and pick him up."

* * *

His son, seeing the results, turned red, turned to go into the house, but Boomer, sitting at the trailer's small dinette table, balled scraps of toilet paper packed up his nose, ice cubes in a dish towel held to the back of his head, said no. And when Gary mentioned the emergency room, he shook his head to that, too.

Gary took him back to his apartment and bathed him, soaking away the crusted blood with a sponge, the bathwater a dirty pink by the time he finished and lifted his father from the tub. Boomer could feel it, Gary averting his eyes, avoiding the weightless, brittle wreck that he had become.

Dressed in sweats, more like swaddling clothes, Boomer found himself settled back on a sofa with pillows and blankets. Gary sat nearby on a rocking chair. A Pat Metheny CD was playing, but the hum inside Boomer's head had accelerated and would not let up.

The CD ended. His son ejected the disc from the player and snapped it back into the jewel case. Gary handed it to his father. Boomer looked at the guitarist on the cover, the words on the back. Gary took his Ibanez from its case, spent a few minutes tuning the guitar, so relaxed, so attentive to detail, less like his father, more like his mother, and then he began to play "Blackbird," a song that Boomer first heard as a sixteen-year-old, stoned for the first time at a party up the south shore in neighboring Superior, at the Broadway Apartments, winter of 1968. Now, forty-three years later, he recalled looking at that blank white album sleeve, comparing it to the vibrancy of *Sgt. Pepper*, and saying, in what he considered a Brit accent, "Bummer," that came out Boomer, which ended up his lifelong nickname.

His son sang the song and played his guitar. Boomer shut his eyes.

"Have I made it to another year?" he asked, his eyes still closed, tired, the fevered hum building to the last chord.

The Forcier Brothers

This was the deer camp on a recent November night: two leaf- and mud-daubed trailers, a weathered plywood plank serving as the breezeway roof between their doors. They were of a late Fifties vintage, so small two large men could not easily maneuver around each other in either.

That night, before the last day of hunting season, light snow began to fall. The small, round-cornered windows were lit a melted butter yellow.

A winter pastoral—obliterated by a rifle blast through the roof of one trailer, a report and flash, the plywood flipped, clattering to the snow-dusted ground.

How did the Forcier brothers reach that November night?

The brothers were a malevolent force in the hardscrabble city where they grew up and then worked in positions of authority. Lyle was a policeman. Clifford, a fireman. In these jobs, the Forciers inspired fear rather than respect in the local populace. Rousting prostitutes at Rye's Savoy Rooms. Terrorizing pimps and basement casino operators at the north end of the city, alley-pummeling informants of any race or religion. Lyle was indiscriminate. Clifford had a yen for women who were victims of fire.

* * *

Lyle wed Pauline when she was seventeen and didn't know much beyond the city limits. A white wedding at St. Stanislaus in the spring of 1958.

Clifford stood as Lyle's best man. Within a year, he was Pauline's.

* * *

Each November, the Forcier brothers hunted whitetail deer amid the birch and pine of northern Wisconsin. They would perch in their separate trees, hunt with their thoughts, and wait for a buck to approach, stop, then walk into the riflescope's view.

* * *

The decades passed. The brothers, pensioned, bloated out of their time, began a life of workaday joes adrift.

In retirement, Lyle with other ex-beat cops at Tony's Bar, Clifford and Pauline would meet. Clifford joked, "Whoever said we couldn't be animals at this age." Pauline laughed, shifted her aging Honey Crisp shape astride him for another ride.

* * *

The brothers drove to Winnipeg, flew to a lodge, and then were flown farther north. It was at the moose camp on Lake Ste. Marie in northern Manitoba where each vowed to kill the other.

Expensive Canadian whisky drunk like water induced a blather only they could understand. Lyle, worrying the possibility of esophageal cancer in his future, said, "Shoot me if I ever come down with that, you miserable fuck. Shoot me like a broken-down horse"—thumped himself with a thick finger between the eyes—"Right. The fuck. Here. Yes?"

Clifford spit out too enthusiastically, "Goddamn right." Then he remembered himself. "And you me, yes?"

"Yes, I will." Lyle lurched back on his cot. "I will take you out if need be."

Passing out slowly, Clifford dribbled out, "Thank you kindly."

* * *

A recent November night. The two are at the deer camp. Lyle was diagnosed in September. He knows this is his last season.

The Forciers drink, recount better days, and this unlucky one. No trophies. Lyle coughs dollops of blood-streaked sputum, shot from between his lips into the unlined wastebasket. Fuck it. Someone's dying.

Both brothers, eighty, eighty-three, have their rifles loaded. A Winchester. A Remington. The waste of the day. Aged knees nearly touch in the tight trailer.

Clifford knew the diagnosis. He could do this, though he'd rather die than shoot his brother. Nothing to do with Lyle. He'd rather die. Die like Pauline. She passed the previous winter. The cancer roved from breast to bone to brain. No word sent to Clifford. He offered to sit with her. Lyle told him no. He could do it.

Lyle's Winchester was ready. They drank shots, toasting long lives. They'd done whatever they'd pleased. He held his rifle between them, the butt on the floor.

Clifford reached a spotted hand for the rifle, but Lyle's grip was tight.

Clifford blinked.

"She told me."

Clifford blinked again.

"She didn't want to go, not with the guilt." He laughed, suffered another scouring cough. "She thought, good Catholic as she was, she wouldn't get past St. Peter with the weight of all that guilt."

Clifford opened his mouth. But Lyle said, "Motherfucker," and fired. The breezeway roof clattered away.

Then, one final blast.

The Hardest Part

The five women, all in their thirties and costumed as pigs in pink cotton onesies, faces hidden by Petunia Pig masks, trotted in through the backdoor of the house on the corner of 16th and Marquette and into its dark kitchen. The one who led them through the unlocked door, Joanne Severson, held a finger up to the lips beneath her Petunia snout. "Shh." A giggle. Then she called out, "Kids, come here a sec, will you?"

Patrick, Kim, Tom, and Richie, this last, the youngest, a purposeful accident conceived in anger on a humid summer night in a Lake Nebagamon cabin, came on the run. Patrick, the oldest of Joanne's four, flipped the kitchen switch. The three circular fluorescent tubes that made up the fixture centered on the ceiling flickered to cold brilliance. The shining masks tilted at her children.

She thinks back on that now, years later. Patrick was the one who turned on the light, wasn't he? He always had. She had to watch that with the other kids. He was the one.

The five women, a bowling team sponsored by Edelstein Brothers, Quality Jewelers and Optometrists, were half in the bag. They grunted and oinked, and then laughed, slapping their pink-cotton knees. The children, the three youngest anyway, with their sleepy grins, were ready to play. But Patrick, Joanne's Book-of-the-Month-Club edition of *In Cold Blood* in his hand, index finger tucked in between the pages, marking where he was when interrupted, looked embarrassed for all these ladies, these adults. They were moms and most of them, though not Joanne, did work outside of the home. This was the exception. There was the one who mixed the dough and seasoned the ground beef in the backroom kitchen at Dominic's Pizza. Another was a Holmgren Clinic nurse who wore a starched white uniform by day, a black stripe across the fold of her white RN cap. And the elementary schoolteacher. She subbed at Roosevelt Elementary, where Patrick went through the sixth grade. All of them were bowlers. He didn't run, squealing and laughing like his sister and brothers, when the bowling team took off after them with their riotous snorting.

The team numbered five. They had all been her friends. Up to a point, Bonita Weir had been her best friend.

She remembers Bonita grabbing Patrick, who was fourteen, a small fourteen, and rubbing up against him until Joanne shouted at her. Later, Harlan, Joanne's husband, said, "Don't mind Bonita. She's just a cocktease. Nothing ever happens." That may have been, but she didn't like a woman in her mid-thirties smushing her boobs into her son's face.

The true and irreversible break with Bonita came when Joanne and Harlan, it was more Harlan, decided to move out of Port Nicollet's old North End neighborhood. "You're what?" Bonita was cooking beef kidneys for dinner when she dropped in. Joanne and Harlan lived across the street in the middle story apartment of a triplex. That late afternoon, Bonita's kitchen smelled of urine.

"You're moving where?" She stirred the boiling kidneys, which she insisted were a real treat, but Joanne thought the kitchen, likely the whole Weir house, smelled like a bathroom where absentminded boys routinely missed the toilet.

"Uptown. Four blocks from Roosevelt Elementary."
Joanne already regretted the move and it hadn't even happened yet. She knew everyone here in the neighborhood.
Over the past eight years they'd rented two different flats
that were only two blocks from each other. Harlan grew up
three houses down the street from where they were living
now. Joanne and her girlfriends would dress to the nines,
heels, the works, and walk downtown when the stores stayed
open Thursday nights, stop at the Elbo Room for a fifty-cent
mixed drink on the walk back to North End.

"Uptown." Bonita said, like the urine stench had finally
crept into her own mouth. "That's rich."

Harlan wanted the kids to be able to walk to school. The
only place better, he told Joanne, would have been a house
right across the street from Roosevelt. None of those were
for sale. She knew he had been thinking, You don't have a
driver's license. She knew he had believed, It will be a safe
walk for the kids mornings and afternoons.

The move didn't cut her off from the bowling team. That
was a good thing. She knew the ladies she bowled with on
Tuesday league nights, champs three years running. A great
bunch of gals in those days. But Joanne knew how nosy they
could be. Sometimes it would make her cringe, wondering
how much they knew about any of those they spoke about.
Who's that sleeping around? Her? Oh, that tramp. She kept
her mouth shut. Whose kid is having trouble in school?
Who's having trouble in the bedroom? The one who didn't
want to have sex the other night, but her hubby did. Big
time. Both feet against the small of her back, he pushed
her out of the bed.

Everything, almost everything had been fair game. But
then, with Patrick, it was all, you know, mum. Oh, they sent

flowers. They were very kind in their Hallmark way. But then they were mum. That was the word for it. And they didn't stop by to visit, like they would taint their own families if they did. As if it would happen to one of their kids if they talked to Joanne.

People assumed that they knew what the hardest part was of all this. They were guessing.

The hardest part wasn't calling Harlan. Those who didn't know might have thought it would have been. He was second cook on the S.S. Pamela Brown. The Great Lakes freighter steamed away with him every year, into November, sometimes later. Once he was gone for 365 consecutive days and earned a commemorative belt buckle. Calling him when he was in the Port of Ashtabula was not hard at all, although she couldn't reach him. He wasn't there. She had to tell his captain and she imagined the captain telling him, making Harlan go quiet, the news bringing him to his knees. But that wasn't the hardest part.

That part about not being there. That was the Severson side of the family all over. That was like Harlan's father, gone when he was most needed.

Harlan's family, a large one, moved from the farming community of Hamburg, North Dakota, to Port Nicollet and the south shore of Lake Superior in the mid-1920s. They lost a youngster back there in the Hamburg area. That loss was before Harlan's birth in Port Nicollet. That older brother, he was buried on the North Dakota prairie.

The child's name was Johnny, and his death would bubble up in conversation with Berit, Harlan's domineering mother, as she entered her nineties. Stroking the liver spots on the back of an onionskin hand, Johnny's story would arrive, carried in, a ghost in her guttural voice.

"Daddy." She called her husband Daddy. "Daddy left a basket of chokecherries on the porch. He left them there and off he went with my brothers, Ole and Nels. Off to town like drunkards will do." She shook her head. "They came back. Ole and Nels. But Daddy, he went off on a bender." The oil furnace in the old woman's living room, it filled a good fifth of the space, ticked with heat. They would wait for her to go on though they knew the story too well, knew how it ended. The little boy ate the chokecherries that his father had left on the porch and grew sick. By the time the doctor arrived, and then, much later, the father, Johnny Severson was dead.

Berit dealt with it.

Her mother-in-law dealt with the loss of a child. Joanne had always wondered how.

The New York-based company that owned the shipping line that the S.S. Pamela Brown was a part of flew Harlan Severson home from Ashtabula. Joanne's brother Andy offered to go pick him up at Duluth International, but she chose to do it by herself.

It was the longest, quietest drive home from Duluth Joanne and her husband would ever take together. Quiet along Highway 2, except for the rushing summer wind sluicing in on them through the open driver and passenger side windows.

But that wasn't the hardest part.

* * *

Joanne screamed, anyway she thought she screamed. Was it at the sleepy-eyed police detective? She thought it was the sleepy-eyed one on the phone, the one who asked her whether there was an adult male relative who could come in. He wasn't even leading the investigation. Andy, her brother, he would know for sure if she screamed or not. He was there.

The hardest part wasn't identifying Patrick, though it started out to be. The police wouldn't, no, they wouldn't let her do that on her own. In fact, they didn't want her to see him at all. During the phone call, someone asked her, and it could have been the sleepy-eyed detective, then again it might not have been, someone asked her, "Is there an adult male relative who could come in?" The police thought it was a job for a man when, here, she'd carried Patrick for nine months and then gave birth to him while Harlan sailed the Great Lakes. Fourteen years ago. Fourteen. Years. Ago.

Andy was there. He went with her to the police station, its entrance at street level, on a side street, not the grand, stepped entrance to City Hall at the front of the imposing brownstone structure. The squad room chatter dropped from locker room towel crack joviality to nothing when Joanne and Andy walked in. One cop, the one she recognized, he was wearing a loud plaid three-piece suit, his sleepy eyes widened briefly, he nodded to them and walked over to a glass-walled office where his partner was talking with the chief of detectives. The plaid detective interrupted the discussion and Detective Blomfeldt emerged from the office.

The morgue, its walls a milky two-tone institutional green, was one level below the floor of metal desks and interview rooms and reached by a hazardous granite stairwell and hallway that reminded Joanne of Roosevelt Elementary and the kids, Patrick, running in the hall at the bell ending the day.

Blomfeldt knew. She knew. It was Patrick on the autopsy table. He was covered by a white sheet to just below his chin. All the clichés came to her. He looks like he's sleeping. He looks so peaceful. Before she could criticize herself for thinking that way, her mind switched: Whatever they did—*Who were they? Why had she thought "They" instead of "He", instead of "She"? Did she even think "She"?*—whatever was done to him that in the end ended his life did not show on his face, his fourteen-year-old face at rest—*his fourteen-year-old face at rest.* Why does he need to rest? He's fourteen. What killed him did not show on his face beyond the purple welt across his right temple and his dark, swollen eyelids.

Blomfeldt looked at her, but Joanne could not even say, "Yes."

Andy settled it. "That's him. That's Patrick."

* * *

The hardest part wasn't telling Patrick's sister and brothers. It was like she was Donna Reed easing the Bailey children's minds when Jimmy Stewart went off in *It's a Wonderful Life.* It was like giving them The Talk, all at once.

"Something has happened to Patrick."

And Richie, of course, was all ears. Kim didn't want to hear it and neither did Tommy. It was like they already knew, hearing Joanne talk on the phone in the kitchen. Hearing their mother, what she had to say. No tears. Anger.

Joanne let the two of them slip out of the room. They would be okay.

They were okay, Kim and Tom. They were, weren't they?

Richie sat on the hassock and listened as she told him, his eyes big and wide.

* * *

The hardest part wasn't telling others, because no one else was around, no one outside of the immediate family and even then, inside, it was not a topic to bring up in conversation over coffee and dessert. It was a violent murder.

She drifted away from the bowling league and continued in the PTA only spottily. Then, through the school group, she met Lynette.

Everyone the Seversons knew had two or four kids. One was rare. Three? Never. Lynette and her husband had four, like Joanne and Harlan, or like Joanne and Harlan used to have. It was what she was missing. Someone like Lynette. Someone to talk to. Someone to talk with about anything, everything, when you got down to brass tacks. Then there was this, after months of meeting over coffee and cigarettes, catching up over the phone. Lynette, opening up to her more than Joanne would have expected or would have wanted.

"Can I tell you something? I couldn't take my eyes off you when I first saw you."

Joanne thought, Oh, and took a deep breath.

"Not true. I did look away when you glanced my way. Do you remember? That February PTA meeting? That February, the winter after? You know? After Patrick? We went out for lunch at Sully's after the meeting.

"I couldn't believe that I'd met the woman, the mother of Patrick Severson. It was beyond what I was used to.

"Can I tell you?"

Joanne felt a sinking. Of her mind. Of her heart. She nodded her head anyway.

"I would drive by your house the rest of that summer and fall, before I knew you, and, do you know, I would not have known you if I happened to see you walking down the street. The photographs in the local newspaper? They didn't do you justice.

"Seeing where you and your family lived on Marquette. Seeing you, Joanne. Seeing you in the school library for the PTA meetings. You, your house, your life. I couldn't see how it touched you. Patrick's killing. Not you. Not the house."

She caught herself. She laughed. Joanne looked at her. The other woman's laughter dying with embarrassed abruptness, as if she finally understood.

But then Lynette continued. "Of course, not the house, but still. You know? Total blanks. I couldn't understand it. How could you go on? How could everyday life go on? I wanted to understand, but I just couldn't see how you did it. "I couldn't see how you, how any of it, could survive." It came out that way, Lynette's words. A flood. Joanne looked on. The blank described by Lynette.

* * *

Time passed. It was like those old movies where calendar pages are blown away by the winds of the season. Month by month. Time passed, flew by. Her children got older. Time passed. But at her core. There. That was where nothing had changed, time had stopped, and it was always the evening that the two police detectives came by the house without calling, came to the front door, the front door used only by relatives arriving for Easter, Thanksgiving, and Christmas dinners, arriving for celebrations. She had always thought that if any of her kids would get into trouble, it would have been Richie. But, no. It was Patrick.

At the core: Patrick met someone on his Sunday morning paper route and that someone killed him.

At the core: Patrick was dead at fourteen.

What was the hardest part?

The hardest part was the sound of him leaving the house that Sunday morning in 1966. Remembering that thump of the solid kitchen door, the slap of the screen door, she could hear both sounds from her second-floor bedroom at the front of the house.

Joanne lived in that house on the corner of 16th and Marquette, four blocks from Roosevelt Elementary, for forty-six years beyond 1966, until her surviving children, at Richie's urging, moved her to Saint Thérèse's By the Bay. And in all those forty-six years that she lived in that house, all of the other departures by the back door, from out of the kitchen and into the backyard and into the wider world, each reminded her of Patrick's leaving that Sunday morning. That was it. The thump of the back door closing followed by the slap of the screen door. The sounds that she heard behind the mask of her face.

It was always that one Sunday morning in 1966.

Suburban Creep

The laptop in the leather bag that the twins, with Myra's help, had bought him for Father's Day, remained on the curved roof of the hybrid until he took the turn at High Crossing Boulevard. Amazing. Yes. It was amazing. It was amazing stupidity on his part.

And now a woman named Spring had the laptop in the leather bag.

"Hi. Is this Trent Gardner?" A youthful voice.

"Yes."

"Hi, my name is Spring Fairchild. I'm so happy I reached you." There was honest relief threaded through the high chuff of her laughter. "I found your laptop bag this morning. On my way into Madison? And I found your business card in it. I don't think the laptop is damaged."

He closed his eyes. First thought: relief that the laptop was not damaged. But how did she know? By pushing the power button? No. If she had, she wouldn't be calling him. "Excellent." Second thought, voiced: "Where can I meet you to pick it up?"

Trent had rushed to get out of the house that morning, running behind, the meeting with the Care-and-Share 2-gether Collaborative board of directors scheduled for eight-thirty, Myra, his wife, asking if he could pick up the twins from t-ball practice at five-thirty. "Sorry, hon, no,"— and then, of course, she wanted to get into it. He cared more

123

for the food shelf and homeless shelter he managed on the city's east side than he did about his own family.

"Hon, this isn't the time."

"When then?"

"Later." Trent walked out to the garage through the mudroom, Myra's response, "I work, too, you know," sparked and faded with the click of the door. His hands too full with the insulated lunch bag, coffee mug, newspaper, and laptop bag, he put the last on the roof of the car and realized it was gone when he reached for it on the passenger seat a half hour later in the Mendota Free House parking lot. What was the breathing exercise Myra had been trying to teach him? Something she learned at the conference for insurance company executives. He was huffing by the time he walked into the board meeting.

Trent met Spring at a coffeehouse on Willy Street. He guessed she had teetered off the peak of middle age a few years before, an apple-shaped hippie in decline with the voice of a twelve-year-old. She exhibited a needy friendliness that tugged a bare smile from the corner of his mouth.

"I'd like to give you something. A reward. But I only have this." He waved the plastic he had used to buy her a mocha breve and himself an Americano.

"The coffee's fine. I'm just happy I was able to locate you."

"I insist. I'd like to send you something."

She looked at him, considering, and then gave him her address. She said it was one of the bungalows on Jenifer Street.

That night at home, everyone in bed, Trent returned from his nightly neighborhood stroll. Myra understood that it relaxed him. It cleared his head to walk the suburban residential streets after dark, to see families, comfortable by all appearances, going about their after-hour lives by lamplight, television light, and notebook light, a seeming surfeit of ease after the day's work was done, unaware of the poverty less than twelve miles away, and unaware of him, peering in from outside. Trent was invisible in his hometown, in this suburban community.

He opened his laptop and dropped down with a focused daze into the image and video files. Digital window peek pictures. The women of the neighborhood in the marquee lighting of their bathrooms, the subdued light of their bedrooms, captured through the space between shade and window frame. Then he opened the video of his first. She begged, but then the nylon cord, too tight, the accident. It had been an accident. He told himself that. The second and the third? Those were not.

And now Trent Gardner had Spring Fairchild's address on Jenifer Street, out of Sun Prairie and into Madison. It was out of his normal range, but he had been thinking about expanding. Besides, what was normal? It was all relative.

The Ice Shoves

Evie knew this about the westernmost of the Great Lakes in winter. When the winds blew out of the north-northeast, Lake Superior's ice surged up against the South Shore until it snapped with a crack like the opening of hell's gate. The ice shoves, as newcomers to the region called them for centuries, shouldered ashore into an unstable ridge of mismatched blocks and shifting fissures that could swallow an adult of most any size. The ridge could well encircle the entire lake. Fragile sheets disappeared, swallowed beneath the advancing mass.

* * *

Cheshire Lane was closing. The COO could see the chain's peak in the rearview mirror. Corporate restructured. The result? Seventy-five percent of its stores peppered throughout the ghost malls of the Midwest were closing. Stu got the call. He tapped Evie and the rest of the crew for the job.

He phoned her first. Evie knew he was repeating Avery's line. Avery was their district coordinator. "Ahead of our work with Cheshire Lane, I think we'd do well to have a planning meeting. Say, a retreat. Make the project planning go down better, you understand?"

Of course. She wanted to ask if he was reading the notes he'd written from his meeting with Avery. But, no. Stu always had the words down cold. The tone and tenor, that was the issue. Drained through the sieve that was Stu, they always came off tentative. Although Stu did press to sound authoritative, that was true. Yes, he was thirty, thirty-one, but his crackly voice was still navigating its way through puberty, the sound of it frequently a hot wire of uncontrolled snaking, popping screeches. Evie rolled her eyes, hanging up. He was out of his depth. When the crew met for the planning meeting-cum-retreat, he would lack a cogent message or any semblance of a preliminary design. That would be Evie's responsibility.

Stu didn't speak out of both sides of his mouth. The sides of his mouth were many.

* * *

Stu, Evie, Lila, Sherry, Marilyn, Nancy, Alicia.

Their job was simple. When a retailer was set to close, the corporate office called them in. It was a fait accompli: the closeout sale. Everything Must GO! Big Savings! Through accounting wizardry, the crew made money, the corporation made money, and Jane and Joe Mid-America thought they were getting away with shopping murder. In fact, the retailer sat back when the crew moved in. The crew pushed up regular prices, listing sale prices higher than the original regular prices. Business, in the end, was good.

The Lake Superior retreat wasn't necessary. But there was the beautiful lodge just east of Cornucopia. All expenses paid. There on the big lake, Stu told Evie, they would have an ice fishing derby. He'd rented deluxe ice fishing *shacks*. "You could weekend in them. Refrigerators, stoves, Wi-Fi, beds. Not cots, but beds."

"One thing," Stu asked, "Have you ever gone ice fishing before?"

She'd grown up in the northwoods of Wisconsin. "Sure. I even have my dad's old ice auger."

* * *

There was the usual pre-meeting round of calls between Evie and the crew.

"Do you remember Rayburn's closeout?"

"You think he would've learned something after a year. What a clusterfuck."

"*Near* clusterfuck."

"We had to save ourselves—"

"Or it would've come down on us."

"Talk about a Stu in the headlights."

"It wouldn't have been so bad—"

"—if he'd just stayed the hell away."

"Locked in his office."

"If he would've just asked."

"Demanding workarounds he didn't understand."

"Afraid this one is going to go the same way."

"Or worse."

"The only thing that works with him is a slap down from Avery."

"We could all make a trip to his office."

"And what?"

"Kill him?"

They laughed.

"We can dream."

The auger. The chasms that could swallow a man.

Evie took it as the crew's blessing.

* * *

Stu was stumped by what he saw. What else is new, Evie thought. The ice shove hemmed in the Lake Superior shore like a miniature mountain range.

"How're they going to get the shacks on the lake?" He wasn't asking. "Avery is going to kill me. The cost."

"Oh, he's not going to kill you." She rubbed his shoulder. "Listen. Before the rest of the crew gets here, we can climb over the ridge and check out the lake ice."

"Really?"

"We don't need those shacks. Come on."

"Can we take your auger?"

* * *

She let him lead. Stu wouldn't have had it any other way. The ridge looked solid to him.

He could have slipped, fallen back on the point of the auger she aimed at his spine, but, like his career, each stumble was forward. With his next to last lurch, he looked back and shrugged before soldiering on. That's when he went headfirst, shocked into silence, down into an open fissure.

But not before he grabbed hold of Evie's hand.

The Effects of Urban Renewal on Mid-Century America

The last time I saw my father was in October of 1972. He stepped from the club in Canal Park and looked up and down the sidewalk. Kenny Franks was a good six-footer, not including the gray-dusted flattop, decked out in a Hershey-brown leisure suit with white stitching at the lapels and cuffs. His shirt was white, the wide collar flapping over the jacket's lapels like the wings of seagulls squawking over a French fry in the near empty lot by the Aerial Bridge.

My mother and her boyfriend drove away with me. They snatched me from the sidewalk where I'd been waiting for my father to come out after making his last business deal of the day. My mother pulled me from that world, left me crying and pounding at the car's window as we passed him exiting the club, looking for me up and down the street.

She met her boyfriend at the steel plant in Morgan Park. That's how things went. They're probably not much different now. People meet people at work who can change their lives. Then they change the family's life. His name was Billy, but she called him Buck, and he told me to call him Bucky or Dad or Pa or anything I wanted except son of a bitch, because then, he said, whipsawing through an Elvis karate move, "I'd have to thrash you."

Forty-four years later, I stepped into the club looking for Kenny Franks. A girl performed acrobatics in the nude on a floor-to-ceiling pole. Expecting to find him there was no doubt foolish, but not any more than believing, if he wasn't there, someone would surely know him and tell me where he could be found.

By 1972, Kenny Franks's world had been crumbling for nearly ten years. This was thanks to urban renewal in Duluth's bowery. Buildings were falling to the wrecker's ball, bars like The Classy Lumberjack, The Spalding Hotel, the places he did his business. Whatever that actually was. I'd heard of three occupations over the years: loan shark, pool shark, and gallbladder trafficker.

New office buildings rose up out of the heaps of bricks and Kenny Franks was pushed out to the canal neighborhood to do his business, to its warehouses, taverns, and strip joints.

My mother's boyfriend drove a '72 Plymouth Barracuda, black top, the rest a beery gold. I chose not to call him anything, at any time. He was how my mother decided to renew her life. He wasn't a loan shark. He didn't trade in black bear gallbladders with sailors on the boats from China. That issue continues in some Midwestern ports, but not as easy as in Kenny Franks's day. Now it's treated like it's a federal crime. The boyfriend didn't deal in illegalities. He fabricated fence posts at the steel plant. "Fabricated." That was his word for it. And he, the boyfriend, the man with the multiple names, was a union man. He busted a number of heads in his day. I hated him. I wanted my father. Kenny Franks.

Although initially I was sure the bartender in the club knew my father, how could he? He was bearded, wore a flannel shirt, dark-framed glasses, and didn't have a clue who Kenny Franks was. The bartender, a kid in his thirties, could have been my son.

The hipster bartender looked at me kind of strange. I looked down at my shirt front, my red hands. I slipped out of the club, much like my father in 1972, looked up and down the street, and came to myself, a fifty-five-year-old who'd gone job to job with a five-year plan to near success. I came to myself, looking at my hands, my shirt, and went back to the rental in the public parking lot. He, the boyfriend, had told me what he'd done to my father. And I knew what I'd done to the boyfriend.

He was in his eighties, out in his garage, working at an emery wheel. His back was to me.

In a corner of the garage was a stack of what he called "liberated" fence posts, cold hard iron clad in green. I picked one up and approached him from the rear. Sparks burst in front of him.

"What are you doing?" I asked.

When he turned around, I swung the fence post down across his face. I didn't stop swinging.

As Good on Him as on a Dead Man

The day that Lucky Penny McAlister's body was discovered, the mercury was flirting with thirty-two degrees Fahrenheit. His death fifteen hours before, give or take an hour, an hour and a half, occurred on a sixty-nine-degree day, a sensible sixty-nine since it was the last day of April. It made meteorological sense. But Sunday, the first of May, near freezing. To be honest, there is no meteorological sense to be made of this city, locked as it is into the extreme northwestern corner of Wisconsin. This rough diamond takes what blows in out of the east-northeast, off Lake Superior, or what rolls on it like a whiskey-dicked drunk, I'm not talking about my ex here, from the hills of Duluth. McAlister, let's say, got caught up in the heat of the moment.

A kid in a heavy parka and shorts, those baggy britches promoting some professional football or baseball team, but now, so drab, a person couldn't say which sport or team, the kid probably didn't know, didn't care, they were hand-me-downs, came bicycling down Main Street on Connor's Point at 9:30 that Sunday morning, past the cement plant and grain elevators, as if it was planned. He found McAlister face up in the weeds near Howard's Pocket, wet snow like rounds of Oreo cream filling covering his eyes, a rust-colored Great Lakes ship at anchor less than twenty feet away.

The kid, straddling what he called his trick bike, was struck by the snowy eyes, the blue cast to the face, the bluer lips. He pulled out his phone. "It's me. Yeah. He's still here."

I thanked him. "Is the ball cap still there?"

There was a pause as he scanned the area. "Yeah."

"You can have it."

* * *

Young men bicycle throughout the city no matter the season or time of day. You might notice this. I did, early on. That it's men, not women. Bicycling. And not on too expensive bikes with narrow razor tires or wearing skintight Day-Glo-colored racing uniforms. No costumes. Street clothes. In winter, yes, some use fat tire bikes, they often ride them year-round, while others prefer the tire chains ordered from Durango, Colorado, or that place in Finland. That is a business expense. The time of day might be when the taverns close, well after two or three in the morning, and then the young men can be seen bicycling to a house party, a girlfriend's apartment, mom and dad's basement, or some other night's squat. It may be the middle of the day. My rule: special care with deliveries, day or night. They have lost their driver's licenses through one too many DUIs or an all-of-the-above selection from the cafeteria plan of driving infractions. They do better on their bicycles. They know the city. They know streets, trails, paths, and alleys. The backyards where no fences will hem them in. They are adept at evading capture. Lucky Penny McAlister was arguably one of the best. One January night, twenty below zero, he eluded the police by biking down onto the frozen St. Louis River, looping in and out of the river's ice-covered inlets.

My Lucky Penny.

* * *

On an overpass sidewalk fifteen years ago, after nearly being run over by a speeding white and yellow GMC Jimmy, he was dubbed Lucky Penny. The recent removal of a plantar wart from his right heel left him limping, but he and his two friends, both stoner Duluthians, made it to the other side thanks largely to McAlister's efforts, The Fabulous Furry Freak Brothers, that's what they called themselves, after a trio of underground comic book characters, swearing at the already gone Jimmy and laughing, relieved to still be among the living.

"You tore ass, man," one friend said to McAlister. "You hadn't pulled us along, we'd all be a bloodstain on Lake Avenue."

"You are a fuckin' lucky penny, man. *Our* lucky penny," friend two said.

"Damn," chimed the first. "Lucky. Penny. Lucky Penny McAlister."

McAlister shook his head. He wasn't one for superstitions or claiming luck as his own. Everything he did was accomplished by what *he* could do, physically, mentally, even at that young age. "Blow that smoke someone else's way."

To McAlister, Lucky Penny was a curse. But the nickname stuck to him, a plain name, like Bob or Joe to anybody else. To him, no. It was a curse.

* * *

He thought he was working under-the-radar jobs, shifting video gambling machines with a loaner Econoline from bar to bar in the county's backwaters, until his rabbity awareness of the Sheriff's Department directed him home, to the city, and the manufacture of synthetic drugs, cannabimimetics, and their sale. I pulled him in and told him that nothing was under the radar or small time. That he would have to pay. Lucky Penny was smart. I turned him as a CI. His talk resulted in convictions. The convictions wore down the competition. It was an easy flip to bring him into the bicycle crew.

Lucky Penny worked the north side of the city after his getaway on the ice-covered St. Louis River. The neighborhood is populated with fixed and low-income residents. It turns lucrative when the Great Lakes sailors are in port. Historically, the North End has always benefited from sailors' dollars. Taverns, tippling houses, basement gambling dens. The red-light district. Money pocketed, police turned to look the other way.

These days, bicyclists, my young men, provide sales and service throughout the city.

* * *

After the call from the kid on Connor's Point, Sunday morning's second call came in from Captain of Detectives Joe Lofgren. I answered, "District Commander Sobczak," feigning sleepiness. It was a day off.

"Anita, Lofgren. I'm on Connor's Point. You'll want to come out here. It's your former CI. McAlister."

By the time I arrived our CSI team, or the one and a half individuals that make it up, the half a technical college intern, was finishing its work. A one-sided conversation roiled my head. I was telling Lucky Penny, on his back and dead, that this is what happens.

* * *

It's what happens after this.

It's something you don't want to hear about from someone in the same business, someone who could turn into competition. We walked on Park Point beach in Duluth.

A fifty-five-year-old woman, a machinist at a garage door manufacturer outside a small Iron Range town, had died. "Did you know?" my colleague asked.

"Yes." It was in the newspapers, on TV and radio. It was hard to miss.

"A fentanyl overdose." Fentanyl. Neither of us use any of its street names.

"I heard that." There had been an uptick in overdoses. The woman from the Iron Range was the most recent. People outside of law enforcement and outside of the trade wonder how that can happen: a fifty-five-year-old grandmother, factory worker, gardener, bowler, blue ribbon winner at last year's county fair for her potato salad, dead from an opioid overdose. It happens. She could have been your retired neighbor. "Accidental," I said.

He shrugged. "Yes and no. She didn't know what she was doing. It wasn't the best."

It happened on the Iron Range. In Minnesota. It was his product. "What are you going to do?"

"I was going to ask you."

I looked at him.

Then he told me that his people had already determined that McAlister made the sale. He was freelancing. Duluth, the Iron Range, rural northeastern Minnesota. Lucky Penny. He was bucking the existing fentanyl and OxyContin trade.

He bounced the question back to me. "What are you going to do?"

Lucky Penny. He made good money working the North End for me. Too good.

* * *

Lofgren finished his preliminary report out to me. The Lake Superior wind blew cold and birders, Connor's Point, though light industrial now, is perfect for birding, left off with their nature activity and with the local news teams crowded the yellow tape.

"You want to take a closer look, Anita, before they take the body away?"

I was quiet, standing apart, but then said, "He always wore a baseball cap. The N and Y were black like the rest of the cap. Did you see that anywhere, Joe?"

Lofgren glanced over the scene. "No." The grass and weeds, thistle, bindweed, burdock, brome, were a uniform dun, flattened by the winter's snow. The fresh overnight traces would leave soon enough. The dirty, ice-hardened patches, they might last until June. Nothing was going to sprout green anytime soon, even if it was the first of May. "I think something like that would've stood out. We'll check along Howard's Pocket."

I nodded. "I remember that he was proud of that cap. If this was gang related," I looked at Lofgren, "The killer may have just decided that the cap looked as good on him as on the dead man."

Lofgren wrote in his pad. "Yeah. We'll follow up on that. Get it to the gang task force."

"You take care of it, Joe. Don't let the state and feds get the credit. We have to take care of our own."

He smiled. "Right."

And I knew that cold May day where in our city the kid in the parka, shorts, and dead man's baseball cap would be bicycling. The particular street, trail, path, or alley. Or, if not on his trick bike, where he would be at rest, earbuds in.

He wouldn't be hard to find.

Mile Marker

Shelley had never noticed them. During her fifteen years of employment with Pinewood Jobs and Training Services, she had worn out over 361,000 miles of tire rubber traveling this one Midwestern state, her home state for all of her sixty-two years. In those 361,000-plus miles and fifteen years with Pinewood, sleeping in chain hotels—smoke-saturated suites though smoking was no longer allowed, spotty Wi-Fi, bottom shelf Chardonnay served up at the manager's reception, tasteless scrambled eggs offered at the free breakfast buffet—working a day or two in this agency's or that agency's training room, she had never noticed them, not once. Never, that is, until last year, during the trip in September, driving roundtrip for staff meetings, from her home on the south shore of Lake Superior to the state capital and back. Then she noticed. The interstate was littered with desiccated deer carcasses. That caught her eye.

Road crews no longer scraped and dumped roadkill in the tall grass and weeds off the shoulder. The whitetail deer, an occasional black bear, wolf, fox, wild turkey, owl, the once living creature that had encountered misadventure on the state highway or interstate, was left where it had bounced for further day-to-day and night-by-night brutalization. What Shelley found strange now: The dead, deer the odds-on favorite, appeared at regular intervals. Buckskin mile markers. Besides the primitive nature of these new mile markers, there was something darkly poetic about them, like Diane Arbus photographs, yet putting her finger on this poetry was problematic.

What it came down to, Shelley concluded, was that, although she was a relatively young sixty-two—she credited her genes, moderation in diet, and, even if attended sporadically, a community college boxing class—she felt as worn and depleted by the tedium of her work as one of those piles of buckskin and bone.

That feeling of having gone beyond her expiration date—she laughed about that one, as if roadkill would have a best-used-by date stamped somewhere between the ears and antlers—would disappear by the time she reached home. Roger, her husband, would have something ready. He always did. He was the City Planner. This was her last trip; reaching home, she would be in out-of-work status forever after. She slapped the steering wheel, one happy woman, and slipped a CD into the slot on the dashboard. The Patti Smith Group turned up loud. Shelley took early retirement, screw the rest. There was never a good time for colleagues left behind, but leave them behind she must.

She wasn't going to just sit on her butt. Shelley told them at her going away party at work. No. She had plans. Besides being a trainer, she had been Pinewood's project manager. And, for her retirement, she had a project in mind. She had been shooting photographs of Great Lakes ships since she was an artsy, patched-jean freak with feather earrings in high school. But photography had turned into a catch-as-catch-can avocation during the long run of her workforce development career, the raising of a family. 1979—the year she walked across the stage and picked up the bachelor's degree that funneled her into the industry of moving people into jobs—was so long ago. Technology had clear-cut the landscape, from her day job to her art. Her forty-year-old 35-millimeter Leica to digital SLR cameras and smartphones. Shelley tried to stay on top of it all. She had moved on to the digital world. The ships she photographed had changed in those forty years. And the bumboats? Were those floating stores around anymore, or did crews order whatever they needed online and pick packages up in ports of call? Her mind buzzed. Shelley's project? A driving tour of Great Lakes ports, and nothing was going to stop her.

Roger worked for the city and didn't plan on retiring for another year and a half, if then. Good thing, she thought, because he could be a royal pain when he wasn't working, say, during vacations and weekends. Her husband would be occupied and, with Shelley's travel, he wouldn't be irritated by her sleeping in because she wouldn't be sleeping in. She would be gone, like when she trained statewide for Pinewood. Roger knew. He understood her longtime interest in photography and Great Lakes ships. She believed that.

Her retirement dinner was a quiet affair. Roger arranged it. Just the two of them at her favorite Mexican restaurant in the near empty neighborhood mall. She talked about her plans, hands dancing over a plate of chilaquiles, building momentum as she spoke. The drive east northeast along Lake Superior, angling through the Upper Peninsula and Sault Ste. Marie, down Lake Michigan, the loop east out of Chicago, clipping Indiana into Michigan, Ohio, and on. The port cities. Always the ports, the lakers and salties. Her husband sat across the booth from her, smiling and nodding. Yes, he was. But he didn't appear to be listening.

Shelley stopped talking. "What's with you?" she asked. Her animated hands came to rest on the table.

Roger smiled broadly, then said, "I'm going to retire, too." The City Planner had plans, and he shared them. Plans for the two of them. Together. He covered her hand that lay stunned beside the empty chip basket with his. Her free hand slipped to her lap. He spoke. There was his 100-year-old aunt in Minot who tried to raise him. And then Montana, where he'd spent his teen years, the ranch for juvies—he shook his head and laughed at his long-gone antics, no one in his office knew. There was his brother in Portland, who, frankly, neither of them could stand—he liked to drink beer and sit on a lawn chair in the garage, watching the world drive by—but still, he was his brother. And Shelley, too. He hadn't forgotten her. She had family in Northern California, Colorado, Texas. "We can rent, or buy, I'd be open to that, one of those huge RVs. We can invite the kids along, if they'd want to join us. Hop aboard at different stops along the way. We could call it, I don't know, The Partridge Family 2019!" Roger's smile froze somewhere in the middle of barreling through Yellowstone National Park. She tugged, slipped her hand away from his. "What?"

Shelley said, "I have my plans. My project. I was telling you—"

"Oh, I'm sorry, Shel. What were they again? I was waiting to jump in with our road trip plans." He licked salt from the rim of his margarita glass.

Shelley took a deep breath and went over the Great Lakes photography project, again, in detail. She liked that word. Project. It didn't include Roger. "Because you're working. You were *still* going to be working. You're the City Planner, for cripe's sake." She caught the waitress and ordered another Pacifico. A shot of tequila, she considered that, too. Talk ground to a halt. Here they were, two professional planners who, until this evening, hadn't shared their plans.

Roger finished his carnitas and fished a credit card from his wallet. He shook his head. "We'll probably kill each other in retirement." He laughed, moving on.

He was up. He was leaving. She hadn't finished her beer. And that tequila, she would have liked that, too. He was across the room. She got out of the booth, struggled with her jacket like she was eighty-two instead of sixty-two. A waitress helped her find her arm. "Wait," she called. Roger was out the door. Shelley shook her head, thinking of what he had said. He might be right.

* * *

In the days and weeks that followed, Shelley watched in disbelief. With her project locked up in the back of her mind, Roger's planning metastasized from the dinner conversation to physical objects.

Although he continued working in the City Planner's office, his retirement date pushed out, the screening and interviewing to be done, the onboarding of his replacement, the road trip mail flooded their home. Tourism brochures and magazines, road maps, coupon books. The mail piled up on the end table by his Scandinavian recliner, and then grew in organized stacks on the footstool and coffee table. Mail arrived from forty-nine states. "Don't worry about Hawaii, Shel. I have a plan for that, too."

She riffled through roadmaps of states she had never been to and said, "You know, there are maps on your phone and tablet, right? I have GPS on my phone." She thought, I'm done with training and slides. If he does a travel presentation, too many slides with too many bullet points per slide, I will kill him.

One Saturday afternoon, he surprised her with a trip to the Vacation-USA RV lot. New and used recreation vehicles.

They took a home-on-wheels for a test drive. The RV seemed a city block long, but Roger drove the beast as if he was born to it. Out of spite, Shelley would have taken out traffic lights, bus shelters, and no doubt a gas station canopy and pump island. The vehicle was all toffee, gold, and white. She shook her head. Roger's face spread into one big beatific smile. "Isn't it a wonder what they can do these days?"

Shelley watched. She seethed, then she stopped herself, wondering, Why am I doing this? Roger wouldn't notice, he was so heavily devoted to his, what did he call it, his Partridge Family Trip.

She packed up her clothing, organized her photography equipment, and loaded her Jeep.

He noticed from the patio door. "Shel? Shel. Where are you going?"

Standing by the open driver's side door, she crossed her arms. "Remember? My? Project?"

He frowned. "You'll have plenty of time to do that." He walked over to her, put his arm around her shoulders. He steered her toward the house.

Or he tried to. "Wait a minute." She whirled from his embrace.

"Let's see how it goes. You won't have to do a thing."

"After all these years?"

Roger smirked. "The trip launch won't be for a few months yet. Take a class. Something in photography. You'd like that, right? Hone your skills?"

Shelley rolled her eyes.

She unloaded the Jeep after dinner.

* * *

She wasn't averse to honing her photography skills. But when Shelley dropped into the Internet rabbit hole of courses offered by every school in the area, she was most intrigued by those at the Lake Superior Shores Folk School, and none of the courses were related to photography. Building a Birchbark Canoe. An Introduction to Apiary Arts: Hives, Honey, and Wax. Make Your Own Rope Hammock. And, this: Sewing with Buckskin. A three-day course.

Sewing with buckskin. That caught her eye.

* * *

The instructor, a back-to-the-earth hipster named Cedar, had a large selection of skins from which to choose. One skin, along with sinew and glover's needles, was included in the Sewing with Buckskin registration fee.

Throughout the three-day course, at breaks, she dawdled at the pile of whitetail skins stacked on a long worktable at the front of the room, her fingers flipping over and between the layers, some hairless, some red-brown, some gray-brown.

"Beautiful, aren't they?" Cedar appeared at her side and spoke as if he knew what was on her mind. The last day of class.

"They are." She considered, then asked, "Would you let another one go? I'd pay for it, of course."

He crossed his flannel-sleeved arms, the open shirt displaying a retro Maxell Tape T-shirt. From faux ponder to big boy grin, it didn't take him long to decide. "I can work that out. One won't hurt the next class I have coming up." He patted the pile of skins. "Pick what you want, Shelley. I love it when folks want to keep up and expand on their skills. Go for it."

She picked a skin whose color reminded her of the ones she had seen on the highway.

Cedar nodded his head. "Great choice. Yeah. No matter what you plan to do with it."

* * *

Shelley called to him from the basement. "Can you come and give me a hand?" She was setting up her workspace. That's what she told him. There was a buckskin laid out across the carpeted floor, the reddish-brown hair side down.

Roger's voice answered, muffled, from a distance, then it came closer to her, from the doorway at the top of the basement stairs. "I said, 'Why don't *you* come up *here?*' I have something I want to show you, Shel."

The living room was dark, the drapes drawn. His ancient laptop was connected to the TV. They stood in the middle of the room. She couldn't believe it. The TV screen glowed with Slide 1, a maddening boilerplate design, a font that changed in style and size from line to line.

With an inspired left hook, Shelley caught her husband on the side of the head. In a slow-motion sideways dive, Roger went down to the floor, but not before taking a blow from a sharp corner of the heavy coffee table and tripping a sensitive remote control. A gurgling came from deep down inside him, then faded to nothing. His presentation began to play.

She watched enough to know. Too many bullet points, too many words. "Goddamn it, Roger."

Shelley massaged her sore left hand as she returned to the basement.

* * *

The overnight traffic at midweek was light. When she felt sure about the location, she pulled over to the shoulder. She hadn't seen a marker in some time, so this seemed as good a place as any. She popped open the back of the Jeep and removed the buckskin-wrapped body, stitched in tight. She laid it alongside the road. At the next exit her GPS recalibrated. Alongside Lake Superior, she continued east, into retirement.

The Price of Copper and Brass

It was important to remember where you came from, to call up at the appropriate time the requisite grit. Nonetheless, Gustafson knew himself to grow wistful, driving in the old neighborhood. The cliché was like a secret code everyone from North End should be able to decipher and know: Don't forget your roots. No matter how distant you wander from that rougher than rough diamond place, recall that you grew up there.

His mother raised her nine children—their old man would sometimes drop by, back in port, off the boats, drunk and abashed, but with cash—two blocks from the shipyard. Her old clapboard two-story was torn down ten years ago by Gustafson, up from Minneapolis for a long weekend. He sold off the salvageable wood to some artsy-fartsy folks from Duluth, and some Ojibwe guys bought the Monarch wood and coal-burning stove. The majority of Gustafson's brothers and sisters now lived in northern California, in coastal cities and towns, and in Ohio, on Lake Erie, always drawn to water, always far from North End. Raymond, the oldest brother, like their mother, was in the grave. Her house gone. What remained, he saw from the alley, was a small residential lot overtaken by seemingly every trash tree and shrub dreamed of in creation, ugly under the sun, or in rain or snow, much like the rest of the neighborhood, the surrounding blocks. The down-in-the-mouth leached out, visible, in different ways.

Rodney, a kid he'd grown up with, hobbled out to the black plastic dumpster by his garage with a large kitchen trash bag. A wan little girl with lunchtime smears of peanut butter and grape jelly around her mouth followed alongside him, twirling an open Powerpuff Girls umbrella. Gustafson rolled down his window, stepping on the brake. "Hi there, Rodney." He nodded at the girl.

The other man smiled, wiped his hands on his dungarees before shaking hands with Gustafson. "My granddaughter. Nancy." He had to be sixty-five, sixty-six, a few years older than Gustafson. Rodney lived on disability from the long-gone steel plant in Duluth; Gustafson had always liked him. Honest kid. Honest to a fault. His smile now, that was questioning. "Patrolling the alley there, are ya?"

Gustafson lifted his eyebrows: maybe, maybe not. "Just up for a few days. Any changes?"

Rodney sucked his lips in like he had no teeth. "No." He took a look down the opposite side of the alley, then back at Gustafson. "Nope. Same old same old."

Gustafson thanked him, said goodbye to the little girl, told Rodney to take it easy, told them both to watch out for the rain.

It was that particular house toward the end of the block that Rodney had glanced at. That house, its yard, was all of a certain North End setting.

Continuing his slow roll down the alley, Gustafson could see the backyard of the place was mud and clay ripped up and churned by wide truck tires, big boy toys, the orange-brown slime rooster-tailed against the owner's garage; the neighbor's garage befouled in the same manner. Gustafson understood the people next door wouldn't complain. And as if anyone would dare trespass on this rutted muck, the owner warned them off with a tire-and-two-by-four barricade—two stacks of tires, at least six feet apart, an old dark two-by-four stretching from one stack of gray-black rubber to the other, a tire on the top of either end of the wood crossbeam, weighing it down. The two-car garage that went with the property, besides the muddy decoration, had its door dented and askew, likely rammed in the past by a pickup truck, probably driven by the property owner.

Gustafson knew these people. They used their world up until it was dead. It didn't bother them in the least. The dead didn't bother the O'Neills. Not one little bit.

* * *

The sky was a heavy, washed-out blue flannel; April, cold and wet, the month when the smelt ran off Wisconsin Point. Raymond should have run. Gustafson's brother's life began roiling that afternoon, forty-plus years ago. He'd been washing his '72 Plymouth Satellite, a sea-green four-door, at a Connor's Point slip. The slip was east of a yard where an arm of a corporate monolith dismantled and scrapped Great Lakes ships past their prime. Gustafson could see the spot yet, all these years later, past the shipyard and across Howard's Pocket, from the old neighborhood alley he eased down.

The way Raymond told it, the two of them in the kitchen of the upper duplex apartment Raymond lived in with his wife and five kids, each man with a sweaty brown bottle of Hamm's, was that he had been washing his car when he noticed the chain. He chuckled. "The chain was looped around a piling, the other end slung tight over the edge, into the water. I'd wiped down the car—it was that sunny

149

day—remember?—so I thought I'd give the chain a tug. It was heavy. Oh, boy." Raymond's eyes *shone like a banjo ringing*, a phrase the older brother often used to describe delight in others.

"Buckets, not just one. I eased them up, one after another." He'd set his beer bottle down on the table, dramatized the drawing up of the chain, hand over hand. "Each of the buckets were full of scrap, copper, and brass. From those old boats, they were busy scrapping down the point."

Raymond was proud of his discovery; his younger brother, thought differently. "Goddammit, you know who probably stole it all in the first place—"

"Fuck them." His eyes widened to emphasize the point. "I told myself, 'Ray, you've got yourself, Ellie, and five kiddos to support—"

"But the O'Neill boys. Raymond."

"Fuck. Them."

* * *

Wet, like the short-straw Jaycee dropping into the Tri-State Fair dunk tank, the sky opened up, and the rain came down. Gustafson looked again at the backyard mire before pulling away. By nightfall, it would be a thick soup.

At the motel across from the steakhouse on Fifth, Gustafson watched the local news. The smelt run was the second story in. The run would peak that weekend, like the night the O'Neill boys got Raymond on Wisconsin Point.

Gustafson thought of the boys now: Arne housed at Waupun; Clifford at a prison in Minnesota; Gene and Lawrence perished one Fourth of July near Pattison Park, throwing M-80s from their speeding car. Stuart, or Stu, still lived in town, a never-to-retire con-of-all-trades.

Growing up in North End, the Gustafsons and O'Neills played football on Rusk Avenue, and baseball too. Swimming in Lake Superior in summer, skating on Howard's Pocket, and the neighborhood rink in winter. Neighborhood kids who grew up together grew up and away from each other, the Gustafsons turning into strivers for at least the middle ground in life, the O'Neills looking to turn the easier buck, they believed, through criminality. The families managed the neighborhood cordiality. They knew each other; they shared a common history.

No one mentioned the copper and brass haul; Raymond's filching of the O'Neills' boodle, no one knew about it, perhaps wouldn't care, as Raymond believed, if they did.

As he had in years past, Raymond went smelting with the O'Neills when Stu invited him along.

Gustafson heard about it later, how the O'Neills got his brother. The O'Neills and Raymond, along with the other neighborhood buddy, Rodney—someone to pass the word: *Don't fuck with the O'Neills*—drove out to the Point for the smelt run.

They arrived late. Everyone was back on the beach, nets pulled in, the small silver fish in washtubs and buckets. Boomboxes pumped out the Stones and Bowie. "Rebel Rebel." Rodney remembered that one. The beer flowed from kegs, cans, and bottles, and the bonfire flames snapped, the driftwood popped, the noisy partyers cast in orange. The O'Neills trotted Raymond down the beach and away from the firelight toward Dutchman Creek, Rodney tailing them warily. The raucous gathering of smelters flickered, a dying star.

The O'Neills beat the hell out of Raymond, Rodney told Gustafson. They didn't have to do the other thing, but they did. "Who did it? Did they take turns? Just one of them? Their leader?"

Rodney nodded at that last: Stu.

He had pressed Raymond's face into the wet sand as if attempting to create a death mask. After he was sure Raymond had suffocated, he had his brothers roll him over. At that moment, a wave rolled in, dissolving the imprint his terrified face had made in the sand.

* * *

Gustafson held open the storm door and knocked, the rain pattering down as if there would be no end to it ever, his boots thick, slippery with mud. An older man pulled open the backdoor, looked back into the house, then joined Gustafson on the back porch.

"Stu?"

O'Neill nodded. He was an old sixty-five, looked like an orangutan with the belly, the long arms.

Gustafson pictured what he had planned for so many years: suffocating, drowning Stu O'Neill in the backyard slurry, packing his nose, his mouth, his throat—choking him. A crowd would gather under the evening rain in the backyards on either side of the mudflat. The few neighbors, old-timers, they would know. They would watch from the other side of the fence, smoking their unfiltered cigarettes, drinking Old Milwaukee. They knew. They wouldn't call anyone.

"I always wondered when you'd show up," O'Neill said. He looked away, peering at the hidden moon, and then his seven-inch prep knife swung up for the evening's opening move, slicing Gustafson to the sternum.

Gustafson folded. He fell.

No one would be calling anyone. Those who peopled Gustafson's dream of this night, they were not there to watch. Only Rodney, standing in the shadow of a garage, holding his granddaughter's umbrella over his head. When O'Neill finished, Rodney turned and walked home.

Uh-Oh, Love Comes to Town

Minneapolis, 1980

Dez, settled back on the apartment's snaggletoothed davenport, weighed his options. Pack his green Dodge Dart, Bev, and escape to Minnesota's North Shore and Grand Marais, or stick around for the long holiday weekend. Splitting for our hometown would leave me with our guests when they pulled in the day after Thanksgiving. Katie and Tricia expected both of us—one, a confirmed long-distance romance, and the other, a prospect. I didn't mind. Not at all. At the time I was a twenty-four-year-old horndog, mistaking that instant-on lust vibe for love, love of the luscious, large-boned Katie.

"Man, Tricia's expecting you. You're not here, she'll steal Katie's car and haul ass up to Grand Marais looking for you." The Jam's *Sound Effects* spun on the turntable. The bass rumbled. No knocks at the door, shouts to turn it down, threats to call the police. Dez and I leaned towards peace, love, and understanding, but were known for swinging the door wide at such knuckle raps, too intense around the eyes, visible musculature taut with paranoia, ready to jump.

He passed the small brass-bowled pipe, coughed, a chugging sinsemilla locomotive. After a slurp of Jack, he said, "She's too obsessed, Petey. I'm not acquainted with that shit, you know? I'm not equipped. I'm emotionally fragile." He did his headshake thing. Moving to the Twin Cities, he was shocked that everybody he met didn't take to his loopy outdoorsman schtick like the Grand Marais locals. A slap upside the head. A community clinic shrink set him straight.

"Yeah, yeah. Fuck that. Tricia thinks you're the love child of a Little Joe Cartwright–Greek goddess one-nighter." I don't know what region of my ass I pulled that from.

"Really? Like, Michael Landon and Aphrodite?" The vanity of men at twenty-four. Caring, not caring, wrapped in that nature of the second guess. We're all pretty much the same, even today's young men. Few admit it.

"Oh. Hell, no. I'm just fucking with you."

He roared my nickname, "English Major!" Then he stretched. "I guess I could stay in town. What would I do at home besides fatten up on ma's turkey day leftovers and listen to my uncle talk up Reagan?" Tricia wouldn't be the third wheel. Katie and I could check the end point of our three hundred thirty-six–mile romance. I could see if it was all in my head.

The weekend began like any of their other visits. Unloading Katie's car after their five-hour drive, luggage to bedrooms, preliminary love maneuvers, Friday night in Minneapolis's Uptown neighborhood, tacos and burritos, pogo-inducing post-punk bands, drinking to excess, and, back at the apartment, ragged Saturday morning hangovers. Through Sunday, it was more of the same. By Sunday evening, Katie and I were puzzling out the end of all those miles. And Tricia? All big wet eyes for Dez.

We left those two spinning LPs—The Clash, The Jam, Talking Heads—and crawled off to bed. The bedside alarm clock ticked off red digits. 10:30. Somehow, naked and only slightly toasted, Katie and I couldn't find each other. The music was loud: "Lost in the Supermarket," "That's

Entertainment!" "Uh-Oh, Love Comes to Town," "Psycho Killer." I touched her, but we were hundreds of miles apart.

"Let's do something different," she said, usually so white bread.

"Like what?" Interest was lit. "This?"

"No. This." Katie chuckled low in her throat.

The bedroom door banged open, the doorknob cracking plaster. She trudged in, strange, bent, backlit by the light outside my room. And quiet. Tricia, slinky drunk. She slithered clothed over the top of the blanket that covered us, then, finally, with heavy equipment noises, she wedged her body between the S-shapes of our bodies.

"Help me." Her other vocalizations couldn't be picked out as one word or another.

Katie turned on the bedside lamp. "Trish!"

Knees and elbows, her forehead, all were shag rug burned, weeping blood.

"Help me," she mewled. "I think I killed him."

Back in the living room, we slammed stock-still—two naked, innocents, the third clothed, seared by shag. Dez was bent at an unnatural angle over the davenport, as though dropped headlong from the roof of our building to the concrete lot below, discovered broken, dragged back into the apartment, flung aside like an old overcoat. An LP continued to spin, the tonearm hiccuping at the groove's end.

I stepped on the sofa, peeked over the side. Pitching back, hand over my mouth like a drama school reject, I asked, "What did you hit him with? A fucking mallet?" The side of his face was mashed. Blood and other matter—okay, maybe that other matter was brain matter and bone fragments, who the hell knows for sure, I was an English major, not a medical professional—congealed on the floor below his battered skull.

"Is…is he dead?" Katie asked. She couldn't act worth a damn either, but I couldn't believe how she looked, standing there without a stitch on, lit by one table lamp. I was quote *responding* unquote. *Sad thoughts, think sad thoughts, dammit.*

Tricia, on the other hand, was a hot mess. "I killed him. I killed him."

I turned on her. "Shut up, we know that. I can *see* that." The wind died in the Bon Homme Woody's sails. "What did you hit him with?"

She shuffled over to the sofa. My best friend had been clobbered to death by this young woman who was attracted to him. I won't lie. I was unnerved, vulnerable to attack, standing on the sofa like the life model for a drawing class. Tricia pointed at the cushion I was standing on.

Rocking back and forth, I felt something odd, something hard. I stepped to the floor and, putting a hand on her shoulder to keep her at arm's length, I lifted the cushion. Katie put an arm around Tricia and pulled her away. Beneath the cushion was a large faux marble ashtray, something from the '60s I'd picked up at a thrift shop. It had been a deep forest green, rectangular in shape. Now it was tacky with blood and broken into three irregular pieces.

Katie gasped. I loved her so.

"Christ, you whaled the hell out of him. You broke up the ashtray. You broke *him* up."

"He said he didn't love me, that he never did. He said he *liked* me. He wasn't interested in seeing me again, except to…" Katie hugged her tight. Tricia wasn't shaking. She leaned out at me. "I wasn't going to be a fucking toy for him." She didn't sound drunk anymore. "I wasn't going to be pushed across the carpet on my hands and knees while he got his rocks off. That was done."

"Fair enough." I wasn't going to argue. There was a lot of rage, her face the color of a sliced tomato.

Katie said, "Let Pete and me get dressed." And to me, "We'll figure out what to do."

* * *

We opened the davenport, Dez's body on the dingy, pecker-tracked mattress, his head wrapped in towels—dishtowels, bath towels, beach towels. Originally a psychedelic explosion of color, they were now a sopping deep red inside a plastic wrap cocoon. I smelled iron in the air. Katie sat on a kitchen chair at the mattress's foot, Tricia sat on the other kitchen chair to the left. I was in an armless rocker on the right.

"If we were in Milwaukee, I'd know what to do," Katie said. She smoked a cigarette, one of Tricia's KOOLs, using one of the ashtray pieces that sat on the floor. She'd already wiped Dez from the chunk of faux marble. It was heavy. No wonder he was dead. She flicked an ash. "Lake Michigan. Chop him up, bag him, weigh the bags down, drop them in. Done. No floaters allowed." She ground out her smoke. Tricia threw her the pack for a fresh one.

"What the fuck are you talking about?"

"Come on, Peter. I'm a personal secretary. I manage an office, I *manage* things."

Tricia's breath caught. "We don't know Minneapolis, though, or Minnesota." Her eyes began to water. "I never thanked Dez for driving us by Mary Tyler Moore's house."

I looked at his body. "He was a good guy that way."

Katie slapped her hands together. "*Land of 10,000 Lakes,* Trish. Remember? On the license plate!"

I was dumbfounded. We had a dead body in front of us and these two were, what, old hands at the disposal of remains?

Since the hardware store wouldn't open until later that morning, Katie sent me to the basement to find a tarp. I hadn't been down there since move-in day. In the midnight hour, it was all dank murk. A bare lightbulb swung each time I singed my forehead against it, each storage unit wavered in the light. Only one cage was locked. 1980. A different time. I found what I needed.

Katie and Tricia hadn't sat around, shooting the shit while I was gone. Dez was still on the mattress, but stripped to nothing but the bloody rags and Saran Wrap skull-swaddle. Katie had me open the tarp down the galley kitchen floor, flattening and banking it against the cupboards on one side and the stove and refrigerator on the other. Anything we had that could cut meat and bone was laid out on the counter. Katie was efficient.

We moved Dez to the kitchen floor.

Tricia had no qualms. Her cry of *help me* had gone by the board. Now she was all, "Let's *do* this!" Katie's hand swept over the cutting tools. Tricia's left hand grabbed the boning knife.

Here I became worthless. I was from northern Minnesota and tried hunting with my old man and uncles. It never worked out. I wouldn't, couldn't get a shot off. I lost my breakfast, lunch, and dinner when the dead were hung head down to be dressed out. Tricia and Katie, they worked like skilled, single-minded butchers. The buzz of an electric carving knife, the squish of meaty handholds, the slicing, sawing, the sound of each maneuver, flipping over a blood slippery thigh, hacking through the spinal column, the thump of a heavy piece of meat lobbed against a growing pile: Without a word, I bailed for the bathroom and hurled my guts into the toilet.

Hunkered down, heaving into the rust-rimmed bowl and looking at what shot out of me—no idea where any more of the waste could come from—I heard a purred sigh: Katie, leaning against the doorjamb. "How you doing?"

I wiped my sour mouth with the back of my hand. "How's it look like I'm doing?"

"Don't worry about it. Trish and I used to hunt every year with our dads and brothers. We missed it this year to come visit you and…" She nodded in the direction of the kitchen abattoir. "We've done this hundreds of times."

"What?"

"Well, not exactly this. I'm talking bear, deer, rabbit, grouse. You know. But I wanted to apologize now." I looked at her. Curious. "We had to use all your trash bags to bag him up. He would've been too darn heavy to lug around in just two or three. Dez was one well-muscled dude. Anyway. Had to use one for his messed-up clothes, too."

Katie got down on her haunches. "I'm thinking it was cutting him up that bothered you, am I right?"

I nodded my head.

"The cutting up—"

"The *dismemberment!*"

Her head jerked back. "Semantics, English Major. We all have to work together to get this right. Together. You following?"

I must have looked dazed. "Are you tracking, Peter? Listen to what I'm saying."

"Okay."

"Trish and I are going to make your apartment look like nothing ever happened. It will be so clean, they'll think— Oh, never mind. It will be nice. Fresh."

"Okay."

"But we have to get rid of..." She nodded again to where, I assumed, the Dez bags were waiting. "If you have any ideas on that particular topic, we'd sure like to hear them because Trish and I, we're just a couple M'waukee girls, out of our own backyard."

* * *

We sat in the living room, the davenport closed up, the women sharing a travel ashtray. Katie was right. For all I remembered of the gore, they'd done a remarkable cleaning job. I no longer smelled blood, not really. There was more the strong smell of Mr. Clean and strategically placed piney air fresheners. The bags of Dez were, of course, unnerving, but I sucked it up and tried not to think of him the way he was. The three of us sat like we were involved in an intervention.

Sunrise would be in three hours. No one yawned. We looked at a map of Minneapolis picked up at a service station. The city of lakes. Cedar Lake, Lake of the Isles, Lake Calhoun—now Bde Maka Ska—Lake Harriet, Lake Nokomis. Fuck me, Minnehaha Falls? I shook my head.

"What do you mean? What's wrong with these?" Katie asked. "It's still dark."

I huffed.

"Were you throwing up?" Tricia asked. "Your breath stinks."

"Stop it. Why *not* one of these lakes?"

It had to be more than a simple dump job. I asked, "What about his car? Don't you think we should come up with some plan? Like, I don't know, he left town? Not just, oh, Dez fucking disappeared, but Bev is still parked outside the apartment."

They looked at me. Katie smiled like some animated night blooming flower of death. "Now you're thinking, English Major. What's your plan?"

I yanked a large 1978 paperback road atlas from the shelf of the hall closet, above the winter coats and boots. Interstates, state highways, county trunks, paved, unpaved, you name it. It was Dez's atlas. He bought it before he graduated from the U of M. He'd highlighted the routes of his young hitchhiker's life, from Grand Marais to San Antonio and San Francisco, to Winnipeg and Nuevo Laredo with a detour to New York City, and back to the Midwest, tramping around Lake Superior and Isle Royale. I loved my compadre. Now I was planning a route to his grave.

On the living room floor, the atlas opened between the three of us to a two-page spread of Minnesota, I noticed Katie looking at me. It was all I could do to stay focused. Lakes. State parks and forests fairly deserted in late November. Gooseberry Falls. Boundary Waters. The Superior National Forest. Too close to Grand Marais. Kabetogama or Koochiching? No, too far to go. But then I saw it. The perfect final resting place.

I pressed the spot with my finger. "There!"

Katie peered. Tricia lit a KOOL.

* * *

Headwaters of the Mississippi, 1980

Katie's brand-new Chev wouldn't carry the body bags. What would be the point? Bev waited in the dark lot behind the apartment building. The temperature was in the teens. There was no snow, not a flake. Katie and I carried the bagged Dez to the open trunk, Tricia stood guard, shivering. Katie was right. Dez was well muscled, a husky cowboy, as he might have said in more together days. A light in an upper story apartment came on as we loaded the last bag.

Tricia was shaky. "Should we check that out?" She'd killed once tonight.

"No," Katie said. "Someone's taking a late-night pee."

It was a clear night, early morning, the city lights mopped up the stars. "Let's get some winter weather gear," I said. "I don't know what it'll be like up north." We gathered parkas, leather choppers, winter boots. Passing the stairwell leading to the upper floors of the building, Tricia glanced over, *Taking a piss? Or watching us load the trunk?* I shook my head.

We left before first light, Katie's Chev following the Dodge with the full trunk. Katie had given Tricia the keys to her car, whispering to me, "I don't want her riding with you. You can be a funny guy sometimes, English Major. That could upset her."

I drove Bev. Katie rode shotgun, head lolling against the passenger-side window. Tricia followed with no apparent issues. We made rush hour in St. Cloud, picking up breakfast at a Mickey D's, then continued on Highway 10. The ride was quiet, the land flat, November desolate, with an occasional grove of leaf-stripped trees by the highway.

The snow began to swirl down outside of Park Rapids, lines of it shimmied snakelike across the pavement. Traffic dropped in both directions. I slowed due to the weather; Tricia and I could keep an eye on each other. The road bent into a deep, old pinewoods. We were on our own with what we had to do. My sense of unease suddenly surged in a massive way.

Katie felt it at the same time. "What're we going to do with his car after we *dump* him, Peter?"

I slapped the steering wheel. "You're the secretary who manages everything. What's *your* plan?"

She slugged my shoulder. "Don't be bringing my words back up to me, English Major!"

I looked in the rearview mirror at Tricia in the Chev. During rest stops, breakfast, she was quiet. Her face didn't show a thing. Sadness. Despair. Resolve. Anger. Guilt. Nothing. It brought out the wiseass in me.

"What about the killer? Think she has any ideas about this? What to do with her true love's car? We're out in the middle of nowhere to dump his body. What do we do with his beloved Bev? He loved this fucking car."

Katie popped my shoulder again. "Would it hurt you to be nice?"

"I promise, she didn't hear a word."

"It's not like she *planned* to kill him. He was a cute guy. Why would she kill him?"

These women were fucking crazy.

"Besides, English Major, you had the brilliant idea of driving up to this middle-of-nowhere winter wonderland to *dispose* of the body. 'We have to take Dez's car! Make it look like he ran off!' That's pretty much what you said, smart guy English major. Use your *English* major to figure out *this* jam."

I choked back a laugh. She did a reasonably decent impression of me.

* * *

In the state park, we rolled along an unplowed road. The snow wasn't much more than three inches deep, but heavy and wet. If we got stuck, we'd have to tramp back to a lodge or gift shop, break in, and find a payphone.

We parked in an empty lot. I took Katie and Tricia walking along a winding, snow-greased footpath, grabbing for tree trunks and branches when we'd slip. The trees spread, the space opened up, and there it was, the headwaters of the Mississippi.

The river was not ice covered. Not too deep, not too shallow, littered with deadfall and boulders of various sizes, some moveable, others not so much. It was perfect. Even Tricia thought so. She nodded her approval. "I could see Dez here. Forever."

"He will be," I said.

Katie appraised the area with her personal secretary's eye. The eye of the fixer. Then she came close, hugged me, and planted one of her wet-and-sloppys. "You done good, English Major. It's beautiful." She pointed out ideal spots for the bagged Dez, placement dependent on depth and whether the bags could be held in place by boulders and downed logs. She popped me a light one. "I think this will come together."

The snow stopped. The sky was a pure winter blue.

Katie and I did the heavy lifting, shifting Dez from the trunk to the headwaters. I hauled each bag into the clear water, far enough out to not be visible from land or the trail come springtime and summer. The water was ice cold and soon I was soaked to my belly. By the time I was done, I was shaking and shivering and my teeth chattered. I thought I would die of hypothermia.

But Katie and Tricia, they stripped me down and huddled with me in the Chev, the heater on full blast. There were blankets in the trunk. A spare change of clothes? I'd thought of those in Minneapolis. They were stowed on Bev's backseat. I would live.

In the middle of the night, a bonfire blossomed in those deep Minnesota woods. Katie and Tricia set Bev ablaze. A perfect touch, because what else could we do? Wipe our prints and abandon it in a Minneapolis neighborhood? No. We left the car burning near the Mississippi headwaters.

The exploding firelight flickered through the branches of the pinewood and shown on the water where, not far below the river's surface, my friend lay in pieces.

* * *

Milwaukee, 2019

I've had to live with that long Thanksgiving weekend for nearly forty years, as have the two women. You're perhaps familiar with a phrase attributed to Sun Tzu, or maybe to Michael Corleone. Sun Tzu said it first. "Keep your friends close, and your enemies closer." As an accessory, aiding in the cover up of Dez's murder, I've done just that with Katie and Tricia.

Here we are in the years, retired and living in Milwaukee, my wife and I, both in our early sixties, fairly healthy. There's been a hot-wire through line of concern all along the way, keeping her close. She's the only one I've had to watch out for. The other? All these years afterward, she began to feel her version of remorse. When we understood this, my wife and I gave each other that *knowing* look. The look that lights up faces when the furnace goes out on a winter's night. *We have a problem and we need to take care of it.*

We took care of it last summer, shortly after giving each other that look. The three of us went sailing on Lake Michigan. Unfortunately for her, due to the weather *that* day, 1980's circumstances, and the onset of her remorse, there was what was officially termed an accident with the rigging and a spar. She drowned in that cold lake, my wife holding her old friend's head under the waves.

Dez disappeared around Thanksgiving, 1980. I reported him missing in December after calling his mother, asking to speak with him, and finding out he never made it north. I was interviewed by the police, as were Katie and Tricia. He'd left after the two women arrived. No. There were no romantic entanglements. We were all friends. He'd gotten a wild hair to pay his mother a surprise visit. He wasn't depressed, though he had seen someone at the community clinic.

I mention the through line of concern, keeping friends close and enemies closer. My wife and I are closer than any other couple we know. For our benefit, I adopted the habit long ago of checking Minnesota newspapers, in print and online, to see if anything strange had been discovered at the headwaters, something stranger than the torched car. Bev made the papers, but nothing came of it. No. I am waiting for the white shinbone or the sand-scrubbed and damaged skull to bob up somewhere along the Mississippi and become headline news in the Minneapolis, St. Paul, and Duluth newspapers: Body Parts Discovered in River.

Then I'll call my wife over to take a look. "He's made the papers, Tricia."

The Cabin on the Lake

Rich Severson hadn't flown into Minneapolis-St. Paul International in years. It had been five years since he'd last been in the Midwest—his father-in-law's funeral in Chicago, his *ex*-father-in-law's funeral. He and Susan had been divorced two years at that point, but the thing was, he had gotten along with everybody in her family, even Susan. When it imploded on the couple—him—Rich was hard-pressed to explain who or what had brought the marriage down. Susan knew. Anyway, it had gone FUBAR, as his father would've said, and his father was one who would've known. Beyond all repair. Crazy. They managed to remain friends.

His coworkers at the sports card shop in San Antonio were surprised that he didn't go home more often, wondered why the trips were so rare, next to never. He would shrug. Rich had taken early retirement and the shop, no longer trafficking only in baseball cards, but expanding into a world of games he gave up trying to understand after a week, provided the level of socializing that he needed when he first moved to Texas. He would have worked there for free.

Eduardo said, "Dude, you hardly ever go back to the Great White North. You're the baby of the family too, right? I thought babies always went home." Eduardo, the shop owner, was a good guy, good people, who loved to give shit to those he loved.

"Where's the science, Eduardo?" Rich laughed. "Tommy, he's my older brother, he goes back all the time. My sister, Kim, is worse than I am. You've got to have that feeling, man. You know?"

Eduardo dipped his wide face into his *makes sense* look.

* * *

After he checks that the hard case is in his duffel and still locked—he has his reasons for owning the semi-automatic, twenty-plus years—Rich talks with a National sales rep and rents a brand-new Chev pickup for the long weekend. Makes sense, a truck for a trip up north—he smiled at that, up north—to Port Nicollet and the surprise his mother had tantalized him with. The cabin.

The cabin? What cabin? *Come up,* she said with a laugh, borderline loony. Rich wasn't sure, pulled the phone from his ear.

He glanced around. Kim and Tommy in the terminal? No. His mother hadn't mentioned them, though if this was a, what, surprise reunion, they'd likely have flown in too. Rich scanned the crowd, cutting through the meandering flow of human traffic, few paying attention to anyone directly in their path, eyes trained on phones, off to find his rental in the lot. He didn't see anyone he was related to in any way.

There was no direct interstate shot to Port Nicollet on the south shore of Lake Superior. From Minneapolis, the route was a Heinz 57 of travel—Heinz 57, a mutt, a mix, a phrase his dad used when Rich was a kid—via interstates, state highways, and county roads, angling up through east central Minnesota into west central Wisconsin at St. Croix Falls, and then north-northwest to Port Nicollet. Some people preferred direct routes. Rich liked this one fine.

He and the sibs were getting up there in age. Kim was sixty-six, Tommy was sixty-five, and Rich was sixty-three.

Their mother was eighty-five. Patrick? There were no more birthdays for him after the mid-nineteen-sixties. Patrick was always a few days shy of fifteen, forever. Damn. Rich couldn't imagine his oldest brother at any other age than fourteen.

He shook the Seversons from his head—no, only Patrick—and swung into Naomi's Munch-n-Run to gas up, buy a Diet Coke, and a package of Jack Link's beef jerky chunks. Original flavor. The cashier, a young woman, tended a baby behind a smudged glass counter of lottery tickets, candy bars, and ads: local softball games, a Fourth of July picnic, a fireworks display, a community fair. The Buddha Baby, what he'd called a chubby nephew when he was an infant, sat in a bouncy seat and slobbered over a white ring of multicolored plastic keys. He assumed the woman was young and that the baby was hers. He said his *Thank you*, thought about purchasing a lottery ticket, decided not to, he never won more than eight dollars. The woman said her *Come again.* As Rich walked to the exit door, he noticed the colored strip on the door frame that marked his height, important, he guessed, if he'd robbed the convenience store. He thought about his assuming the cashier's youth and if her siblings, if she had any, still thought of her as a child and where she fit birthwise in their family lineup. He was going to turn back and ask her this and more but didn't want to frighten her with his oddball questions. He knew his family, and that was about it. The kids, all in their sixties, still performed the same roles—he rolled his eyes, started the pickup truck—the roles allotted to each of them in the middle of the last century.

* * *

His mom, Joanne Severson, was full of surprises. First, the phone call to come north for this out-of-the-blue weekend rental, whatever it was, the cabin. Second, when he pulled in at Saint Thérèse's by the Bay—the assisted living facility he had persuaded her to move into, away from the big family house at 16th and Marquette, its emptiness—she was waiting in the lobby, antsy for the ride to Lake Nebagamon.

Rich asked, "Can I at least use the bathroom before we roll?" She groused all the way back to her unit at the far end of the building. "No hurry, right?" Joanne flashed her *Get your rear in gear* look.

Stepping from the bathroom, he clapped his hands, *Here we go.* Joanne was all amiability with the echo of a distant chuckle. She finished off a quick vodka-rocks and rinsed the glass in her kitchen sink.

"Okay then," Rich said. "Shall we hit the road?"

There was little chatter, no catching up out on Highway 2 and south on County Road F. Joanne was happy. She tuned in a talk radio show from the Twin Cities—"I never miss it."—whose host was a conservative, no denying that, although he repeatedly voiced his opinion that the reality-TV president and his sycophants were riffraff of the lowest sort. Rich thought the host was that rare animal, what he would call a *normal* Republican.

He glanced over at his mother. Sure, they hadn't been together too long today, but she gave off no signs of Uncle Andy, her kid brother. Not that Rich could tell. Andy's last few years had been awful. Senile dementia. His mother? He believed hearing was her big issue.

Not Joanne. Though in denial about the quality of her aging ears, she punched up the radio's volume for her program, and turned it down whenever a commercial break choked off the radio gab. Squelching advertisements was Joanne's sixth sense. Rich took the opportunity to ask questions.

"You said this is Harry Wicklund's cabin on Lake Nebagamon?" A vague memory of Wicklund surfaced. A tall, pleasant man with wavy black hair molded into shape with Brylcreem, the start of gray over his ears, in a short-sleeved white shirt, no matter the weather, black pants, and a grocer's white apron. He owned the only grocery store in Port Nicollet, at least until Red Owl moved into town. Now few remembered Wicklund's small operation and mourned the passing of the Dirty Bird, buying T-shirts and hoodies with the chain's retro logo at record stores and online.

He thought she heard his question. She nodded.

"Is he going to be there? Kim or Tommy?" He gave her a quick look, smiling.

Joanne shook her head. "No to both of those questions, Mr. Curious."

"So why? What's up with Harry Wicklund's cabin?"

Talk radio loomed, returned. She heard the burble of voices and cranked the volume. Rich eye-rolled a whatever, watched the curving blacktop, enjoyed the brilliant green of the northern Wisconsin woods.

Another commercial break, radio on the down low. She said, "He left us the cabin."

Rich didn't stomp on the brakes or swerve off the road, but he looked at her, sharp, questioning. "What the hell. Why?"

Her facial wrinkles did the shrugging for her.

"When did he die?"

Her show came back on.

His eyes widened at the zero sense of it all.

* * *

Rich had entered the rural route address into his phone and the woman with the silky British accent—reminded him of

Diana Rigg, the jumpsuited Mrs. Peel—directed him turn by turn. And soon they were there, at Harry Wicklund's cabin.

He parked on a small lot made up of hard-packed dirt and gravel; the few spots had railroad tie parking stops. Like Joanne had said, no one else was there. Harry, of course not. And no Kim. No Tommy.

The dark, dense woods in front of them, the heavy shadows, suggested a dream from the Brothers Grimm, the dead man's cabin—*He left us the cabin.*—invisible from where they sat in the pickup. He had questions, but this one seemed to him most pertinent. "Was I here before?"

His mother pursed her lips, appeared to think his question over, then chose to ignore it, climbing from the pickup. "It's down the hill there, through the trees."

The mix of tamarack, balsam fir, paper birch, and popple made for a shadowy climb down, a stairway built into the hill with more railroad ties, each at a different stage of decay. He helped Joanne along, his hand at her elbow. They stepped into a cool, humid clearing fringed with ferns, the trees allowing only a glimpse of a crooked finger of clear blue sky above their heads, the cabin set on the far side, its brown-stained timbers black with age. Two Adirondack chairs and a small table sat near the cabin's door. *Harry's Castle*, burned into a three-foot-long plank, hung over the white screen door.

"I don't get it," Rich said.

Joanne stood with her arms akimbo, a pose she must have copped from a movie. "Isn't this"—she strained for the word, he knew she did—"grand?"

"'Grand?'" He smelled mold and wasn't sure if it came from the surrounding woods or the building. The cabin looked like it had shouldered its way past trolls and witches

to hunker down at the edge of the clearing. Long ago, someone—Harry?—trimmed the cabin's four-paned windows in
white paint, matching the wood of the screen door, and they
hung, bright in the dim light, tucked into the cabin's dark,
timbered walls. He smelled time. He saw its passing. The
roof's shingles thick with moss capped the scalloped fascia,
a continuation of his premonition of fairytale horror. In
shadowed corners and crevices, spiders had spun kingdoms.

"When did Harry die?" It was familiar, the clearing, the
cabin. "Why would he—"

Joanne didn't hear him, disregarded him. One of those.
In three strides, she was at a terracotta pot of red geraniums
by the cabin door. They were fresh, the color of the flowers,
taken care of. One hand against a cabin timber, she shifted
the pot to retrieve a key. She waggled it at her son: the key
to the prize.

He gave her a bemused look. "Ah, mom."

"Watch your head there, Rich." She was still a tall woman.
They both ducked entering *Harry's Castle*.

He noticed the smell from outside had followed them
in, or was there all along, that old cabin smell: wood rot,
mold, damp books, lingering odors of meals long gone.
Inside the door there was a homemade chest and a bin
filled with boots, shoes, and flip-flops. The small living
room had two three-foot tall bookcases, golden wood, New
England kitsch, loaded with Louis L'Amour westerns and
Avon and Dell paperbacks, who knew what they were about,
and a few framed photographs. "That's Harry and his wife,
Germaine," his mother said, nodding at the pictures. "She
died. Did you know that? Young. Poor thing." There were
two padded rocking chairs and a loveseat upholstered in
matching, likely scratchy, black-to-brown-to-cream plaid.

On a small wooden television stand—Rich guessed it was an L. L. Bean purchase—sat a portable TV straight out of the eighties, a ball of tinfoil on the tip of each rabbit ear.

Joanne moved on to the kitchenette—reds and whites, early sixties—and was grinning, going through the drawers.

Rich whistled. A VCR. A portable stereo-turntable setup. An 8-track tape machine with a stack of blocky tapes—country, forties big band, fifties pop. A cassette player-recorder too. Harry apparently had liked his electronics.

"What a mishmash. How old is this place?" Rich asked.

Joanne glanced over her shoulder.

"How? Old?" he repeated, louder.

She said, "It's sweet, isn't it?"

He shook his head, wanting to ask, "Did you hear me? What are you thinking of?" but instead asked, "Two bedrooms? Through here?"

She followed slowly, nodding, hanging back.

"Which do you want tonight?" He couldn't see them staying more than one night. It was feeling like one night would be pushing it. "I suppose you should get the master bedroom, or should I say the *mistress's* bedroom?" Rich bowed, swung out an arm.

Her eyebrows lifted. Her lips pursed.

"Okay, okay," he said. "Madame's boudoir."

That was better. A little bit.

* * *

Rich brought his large duffel and Joanne's suitcase and cosmetics case—a small pharmacy of meds—down to the cabin. There was a woodstove that she wanted to fire up that night, so she asked him to chop wood. She directed him out around to the back of the cabin where he found a woodpile, a stump, and an ax. Directly behind the cabin, down the slope and through the trees, he could see a small, weathered boathouse on the lakeshore.

He imagined he'd been here, perhaps as an infant. That was possible. His ex-wife remembered flying as a baby with her family to Los Angeles. Wait. He chopped. Maybe he did recall his sister and brothers talking about this cabin.

"There was this time each summer when we would spend a weekend in the woods on Lake Nebagamon. Patrick watched us." He remembered Kim telling him. "The parents all got crazy. I think they were all drunk."

"Even the moms?" Rich asked. He had been a wide-eyed kid. He always wanted the whole scoop.

"Yes, even the moms. And they went swimming."

"Drunk? And swimming?" Rich remembers Kim's description. Vivid in his little boy mind. He could see it, smell it, as if he'd been there.

"Yes. Skinny-dipping."

"Skinny-dipping?"

"Naked. All the moms and all the dads. Patrick told Tommy and me. He played Daniel Boone and snuck up on them."

"He saw all the naked moms?"

"Yes. And dads." Kim had looked around, made sure they were alone. "Some had erections."

At that age, Rich didn't have the language down, let alone the mechanics of human sexuality. Erections? A roll of the eyes. Oh, those. He had no idea beyond Erector Sets. Kim nodded slowly. Patrick, a six-year-old, was sure to share all the gory details with bug-eyed Kim and Tommy. No one goes looking to see their mother as a wood nymph.

Rich snorted a laugh as he finished his wood-chopping chore. That's how he knew this place. From Kim's stories when he was a gullible little kid. He glanced down at the boathouse before he filled his arms with wood. He'd have to check that out later. Naked moms and a parade of Erector Sets. A Fellini film relocated to a northern Wisconsin lake. It cracked him up.

* * *

They had grilled hotdogs and Joanne's potato salad—salad dressing, not mayonnaise—for dinner at the small table in the kitchenette. She brought her low-shelf vodka and drank it on ice. Her children tried an intervention twenty, thirty years ago. Its intended purpose failed at everything but tears and accusations of backstabbing. She continued with her vodka-rocks; Rich was sober twenty-five years.

She had unpacked his duffel bag when he was chopping wood. "What's in that locked up metal case? I love these Nathan's hotdogs, though I can't see competing in an eating contest, shoving them down my throat."

Mom. He shook his head. "Yeah, they're not bad. It's my pistol. I told you I had one. You don't remember?"

Her eyebrows rose for *no*, a shake of the head for emphasis. "Because of Patrick?"

"No. I don't think so. Easy to say yes, but no." He swabbed his plate with an inch of dog and bun. "I told you. I thought I did. Why I got one?"

She could belt the vodka. She licked her lips. "No. You never did. Then again—" She tapped the side of her head with a finger. He caught that, nodded.

"When I lived in Minneapolis. In the eighties. I was out late, downtown. Cutting through Loring Park on my way to my apartment, I was mugged."

"Hm. You want another *Klar*-brunn?" She laughed. "I wonder why anyone would pay for a can of water."

176

He ignored her wonder. "No thanks, I'll float away. So, yeah. I was mugged. I gave the SOB everything I had on me. He sucker-punched me, knocked me to the ground. Then he ran off."

Her eyebrows again, *What?*

"He had a gun. He had a knife. After all these years, I don't know for sure what he had."

"More potato salad?"

He glanced over, wondered if she was on some other track. Uncle Andy crossed his mind. "A little." He pushed his plate forward; she spooned more on. "Thing was, I'd cooperated with the guy and he still slugged me. That's why I got it. The gun. I decided I wasn't going to let that happen again." He shrugged.

"Has it?"

"Not once. No muggings, no anything. But I've kept the gun. I'm keeping that."

She nodded, this woman who'd lost a son to homicidal violence fifty-three years ago. "A good idea. Maybe you could show me how to use it tomorrow."

He looked at her, thought about that. "If you'd like."

"I'll clean these up later. Let's go start a fire."

* * *

The family buried his brother in Greenwood Cemetery and later, grudgingly, his mother took care of the arrangements there for his father. The last time Rich was at the cemetery he spoke to their graves.

Sitting by the woodstove, he thought of his father. He would have turned a hundred years old the previous February. "I don't think I ever knew dad. You know what I mean?"

Joanne rocked. "He was never home."

Rich nearly lapsed into the usual, *He was and he wasn't for much of the year.* But he veered off. "I think I'll stop by Greenwood after I drop you off."

"Say 'hi' for me."

"I'll do that. Say, did you bring Harry's will with by any chance? I'd like to read it."

She smiled.

"Mom?"

"No, I didn't. I looked for it, but I couldn't find it." Then she laughed, repeating his words. "'I don't think I ever knew dad.' You did and you didn't. That's for sure."

"Yeah. You're right."

She rocked. She smiled. The woodstove lit them burnt orange. Joanne covered a slow blooming yawn. "I'm going to bed." She got up, hugged him, kissed his cheek. Then, knowing her way, disappeared into the dark beyond the woodstove's glow.

* * *

Rich woke up sometime after two-thirty in the morning and it was black and quiet. The quiet. He listened. He couldn't even hear wildlife prowling the woods. He would have preferred that. The quiet bothered him; the quiet was a vacuum, all life sucked from it. He tried reading—a Tana French novel on his phone—but that didn't work. He couldn't get into the story, and it wasn't putting him to sleep. He looked out his window and, when his eyes adjusted, he could make out the black outline of the boathouse, down on the shoreline.

His phone's flashlight led the way. There was a path at one time, likely better at that time, though not too overgrown now. The mosquitoes. They bothered him, buzz diving. He thought of going back, slather on the bug dope, but continued, eaten alive. He could see himself at sunrise, welts upon welts from the mosquito bites and who knew what else—poison ivy? He would check Harry's medicine cabinet for calamine lotion. Rich questioned his late-night walk, doubted the rationale for it even more when he heard the noise from down by the boathouse.

He stopped and listened. Raccoon, fisher, marten? Black bear? He swept the flashlight beam across the boathouse, less than fifteen feet away, and the noise grew, something excited when the light passed over the windows of the double doors facing him. No animal ran and none lingered, waiting for him.

"Damn mosqui—" Rich swatted and jettisoned the phone. He thought he heard it land, the flashlight beam aimed down. Pitch black. "Goddammit." He crouched down, patting the ground, looking for the dim screen.

Then he heard it, a soft, mournful sound: "Help. Me." Distant. A cough, faint, and another: "Help. Me," and, "Please?" It came from behind a closed door.

Finding the phone, he latched onto it and swung the light back up on the boathouse. Hunkered down, he called, "Hello?"

He held his breath and listened and it felt like the lakeside woods listened with him. He tried again. "Hello? Where—"

"Help. In here."

Rich walked up to the boathouse's doors, taking a quick look behind, then right and left. No one around him. Not his mother checking on the noise, as if she could have heard it. No one. The doors, doubled like on an old garage, each had four panes of glass in the upper quarter, some cracked, all gray-fogged with cobwebs and time.

A padlock hung from the door's hasp unlocked. Rich's light pressed against the window glass bounced back at him.

He lifted the padlock off and pulled a door open. It ground against the sand and dirt, the building having settled over the years. He swept the empty single slip with the flashlight, a dock on either side of the night-black water, a pulley hoist. And, finally, an old man, slumped against a wall, tied up. When the light hit him, he jerked as if touched by an electric prod and Rich did the same. Then the old man shied away, unsure of who was behind the beam of light.

"Shit!" Rich said, walking up to him. The old man tried to smile, but in the end it was impossible. The corners of his thin-lipped mouth bowed down, his eyes welled up. "Shit, hey, don't cry. I'll get you out of this."

"Thank. You."

Rich gagged, working the knots loose. The old man said, "Give yourself a break. Get some fresh air." He sobbed. "I shit my pants. My ass hurts like hell."

Turning his face away, Rich took a deep breath, then turned back to the work. The rope knotted at the man's wrists and ankles was like the work of a child new to it, tying through loops and twists, over and over, one atop another. They might have come loose easily enough—it was surprising the man hadn't twisted himself free, however long he'd been there—yet Rich still had to work at undoing each knot.

"I never thought anyone would hear me," the old man said. His hands tied in front of him, he was able to reach a water bottle that leaned against his thigh. "I've been saving"—he slugged down what remained—"that last swallow, hoping someone would come." His voice like tumbled gravel, he looked tired, relieved, and he could smile and was happy to.

"I would hear boats go by, speed boats—the dock would rock here, that surprised me—and people talking, talking probably across the lake, but it sounded like they were right outside the boathouse. Same with ball games on the radio. Across the lake, but sounded like the radio or TV was right outside the door there."

He rubbed his wrists and ankles, sat gingerly on his self-described crap-crusted rear end. The man wore a Packer-logoed green fleece over a plaid shirt, and khaki trousers. His feet were bare except for white compression socks. "Took my sneakers. Keens." He shook his head, thick waves of white hair. "I thank you so much."

"No," Rich said. "I'm glad I found you. I couldn't sleep. Got up. How long have you been here?" He remained crouched down by the old man. Sure, the smell was outrageous, but, strangely, Rich had grown used to it.

The man put out a gnarled hand covered with wiry white hairs. "How long? I think three days. Name's Harry Wicklund"—they shook hands—"This is my place. The boathouse, the cabin up there."

Harry Wicklund. Rich eased himself down. "I'm Rich Severson."

Wicklund's face took on a tic, a corner of his mouth indecisive about going up or down and remaining there. "Thought you looked familiar. She here?" He bit off the last two words, then he went quiet. From fear or reluctance, Rich could not tell.

"My mom?"

Wicklund nodded. His jaw clenched, Rich could see the roll of jaw muscle, the grinding of teeth.

"Yes, she's back at the cabin. Sleeping." He got to his feet, arthritis skittering painfully in his left knee, and leaned to help Wicklund up. The old man pulled away. "Let's go up there, warm you up. Find out what's going on." Rich smiled, as much to say, *Look at me. I'm harmless. No danger.*

Hand over hand, rolling to his knees, hand over hand, up against the boathouse wall, Wicklund managed to get to his feet on his own. He appeared winded, and Rich thought fired up too. The old man said, "I'll tell you what's going on. She. Tied. Me. Up. Left me here." His face crumpled under his knobbed hand. He leaned against the wall.

Rich, mouth hanging open, put a hand on Wicklund's shoulder. "I'm, I'm sorry."

Wicklund's hand wiped at his eyes, his runny nose. He hiccupped after the tears. "Rich?"

"Yes?"

"Tell me the truth now: Are you in on this with her?"

Rich shook his head.

"Because, if you are, goddammit—"

"No. Christ, no. I. I don't, what—why did she do this? What did she say?"

Wicklund dug in a back pocket for a handkerchief. He'd stained it. He swore and tossed it aside, then, leaning over, blew his nose into the slip. Wiping his hand on his pants, he nodded and then shook his head. "I'm ashamed she'd think such a thing. That I was involved in that, *that*, what happened to your brother."

Rich stepped back.

"Wait. It is *not* true, I swear to God, to whatever Joanne wants me to swear to. God. My wife, Germaine. My mother." The old man choked up again. "I could never. Never."

Rich placed his hand against the wall—he needed to— between antique orange life preservers and worn wooden paddles. "Why would she think that?" It was all too much: the cabin; Harry Wicklund leaving it to them; Harry Wicklund not dead; Harry Wicklund alive; Harry Wicklund tied up in his boathouse by his mom; his mom accusing

Harry Wicklund of having a hand in Patrick's murder. "Why shouldn't I believe her?" he asked, thinking, *Why should I believe her?*

Wicklund shook his head. "No, sir. Dammit." He wiped his nose, wringing the nostrils between his thumb and index finger. "Okay. I don't, I never wanted to tell you this under any circumstances. And here, this."—his hands spread wide, taking in the dim boathouse, the phone's light—"I know *she* never told you."

Rich felt his pulse thrum, his shoulders sag. "Say it. Say whatever."

"I believe—No, goddammit. I *am* your father."

* * *

Back at the cabin, Harry Wicklund worked off his socks, the bottoms covered with pine sap, needles, and dirt. Rich considered carrying him up the slope from the boathouse, but he was too tired, mixed up, angry too. It was enough to guide him, one hand clasping his stringy upper arm, the other lighting the path with the phone. The sun was rising; the woods were dim.

Wicklund cleaned himself in the tight quarters of the cabin bathroom and Rich loaned him fresh underwear, jeans—the old man rolled up the cuffs—and a San Antonio Spurs T-shirt. Rich's eyes ran across Joanne's bottle of vodka on the counter, but, no. Overtired, he stood in the kitchenette. Harry Wicklund sat, eyes on the empty TV screen, hands on his knees.

Joanne, in a just-up fog, patting the pockets of her emerald velour robe zippered to her neck, looking for her BIC lighter and the pack of Merits she'd cold-turkeyed in the eighties, walked down the short hall from her bedroom to the living room and kitchenette. "Coffee on?"

"No." Rich nodded to the man seated in the plaid-upholstered rocker. Joanne glanced over, still hunting for her cigarettes and lighter.

Wicklund looked back at her, sighed, and turned away.

Rich expected something, but this wasn't it. Joanne smiled and raked her short gray bob, fluffed the bouffant that was no longer there. "Hello"—she turned to her son—"Put on a pot of that Scandinavian blend, would you? That package from Arco."

To Wicklund, she said, tilting her head to better see his face, "You're familiar. And I love your wavy hair. I *love* that."

Stiff after the days and nights in the boathouse, Harry Wicklund pushed himself upright, straightening out the kinks, and faced the Seversons. He took a deep breath, puffed out on the exhale. When Harry had collected himself, he ran a hand through his hair, then said, "Hello, Jo."

She frowned, though it was not unfriendly, more out of curiosity.

Rich, who hadn't gotten to the coffee, said, "This is Harry Wicklund. Harry. Wicklund."

Her eyebrows lifted dubiously.

Wicklund eyed Rich, then Joanne. "We've known each other for years. Sixty, sixty-five years."

"You're a good-looking man, but..."

Wicklund shook his head.

"You look like Harry Wicklund's father."

"No. I came here, to the cabin. Last week. You were here. Remember?"

Joanne nodded, but for Rich there was some absence. She wasn't agreeing.

The old grocer coughed a laugh, stopped abruptly. "Anyway, yes. You were here. Surprised the hell of me. I guess I could say you got the drop on me. I don't know if it was your thinking"—he gestured at Rich—"about Rich here, or Patrick." He rubbed his lined forehead and looked down. "You got me down to my boathouse, down there. Tied me up."

Joanne looked at her hands. No BIC. No Merits. Then she asked her son, "Is that coffee done?"

Rich mouthed an *Oh* and turned reluctantly to the coffeemaker.

She turned back to the old man. "Harry Wicklund was a black-haired man. He owned this cabin. He had money and parties. A wealthy widower—he could've had, maybe *did* have anyone he wanted. Anyone. All of us here for his summer parties. Anyone of his friends and neighbors. Probably did anyway."

Wicklund shook his head, said softly, "No. I'm sorry, but that's not true."

Her eyes had seemed distant, now their focus tightened on him. "I wonder who it was then on any weekend before or after. Bonita? That tramp?" Her hands squeezed the pockets of her robe. "I always thought Harry slept with every single one of us on the bowling team. Sure. He wanted to *sponsor* us. Sure he did."

"No. I'm sorry, but no."

Their conversation ramped up this way, a one-sided call-and-response. Rich left off with the coffee and leaned against the kitchenette counter. He watched and listened. No give and take, only accusation, denial, and apology, but for what? The apology was never enough for his mother.

"It wouldn't have happened if he hadn't taken me in there." She pointed to a bedroom.

"I'm sorry."

"He'd say it was because I was drunk."

"No. Yes." He shook his head to clear a view to the past. "We both were."

Looking at Rich, she said, "He didn't wear a condom."

Harry wiped his eyes, a pinch of his index finger and thumb.

"Tell me your birthday."

Rich jumped, told her the day in March of fifty-six.

Joanne repeated the date. "Do the math. I got pregnant in the summer of nineteen fifty-five. My *husband* was sailing on the Great Lakes, working on an iron ore carrier. Do the math."

Rich looked at her, looked away, and looked back again. She sounded younger than her eighty-five years. Plainspoken. He wondered how he'd reached the age of sixty-three without questioning, or, as she said, doing the math.

"In March of fifty-six you were born."

She hadn't finished. It was like the run-on monologues his Uncle Andy ripped through when coiled deep down in his dementia—the dark funhouse of glass and mirrors, smoke and searchlights, the life of wrongs and half-remembered grudges that Andy traversed. Was his mother there now? She could look away, then turn back and not recognize he was her son.

"Then the worst of it began. Harry Wicklund wanted to give me money, like I was a whore. Because he knocked me up."

"Joanne, no. He was, *is* my son. I wanted to help. In any way that you would've wanted. I knew you were Harlan's wife. I. No, I'm sorry."

"Harry Wicklund thought he could pull me in. Money. When that didn't work, violence—"

"No, I'm sorry. That's not true."

"Violence. Against my family. Take away my other children, by whatever means, one by one. Except for my baby. Rich."

"Mom."

"Harry Wicklund killed Patrick. Harry Wicklund would have killed Kim and Tommy. If I had a pistol, I would shoot the son of a bitch."

Rich thought of his gun, thankful he'd kept it locked up. "Mom."

"No, I'm sorry, but no," Harry Wicklund said. "That's incorrect." Tears ran, but the old grocer's voice remained steady.

Rich, arms crossed, the smell of coffee filling the cabin, watched his mother. He could see it, the dark fun house she wandered, room after room.

"Mom, we have to leave. Why don't you go back to your room and get dressed?"

Harry Wicklund was his biological father. Rich believed this to be true.

Harry Wicklund had not murdered his brother. Rich believed this too.

Joanne turned her gaze to her son. "Could I have a cup of coffee first?"

Rich frowned, opened his mouth, but before he could say the word, shake his head, Harry Wicklund spoke.

"Yes. Yes, you can, Jo," because, after all, it was Harry's Castle.

Playdate

Drallmeier listened as the voice on his phone directed him to the elementary school's playground. His four-year-old nephew, Jackson, whined for a cold juice box.

"Not now, man." He took a wrong turn and the app on the phone recalibrated. He squeegeed his bald, sweating scalp with the palm of his hand. "When we get to the playground. Now keep it down so I can follow the phone's directions."

He was driving from West Duluth, where he lived with his sister, Tina, and Jackson, to a school's playground in some residential area of Superior. Over state lines. Minnesota to Wisconsin. He was hoping Clifton's plan was a good one, that the man had turned a corner. Drallmeier hoped.

* * *

It was late June. Summer vacation. From the curb, he could see the playground, empty except for the swings, the jungle gym, a merry-go-round—Drallmeier remembered a curl of puke flaring from his mouth when he rode one for the first time as a kid—and cartoonish creatures attached to thick springs embedded in the ground. All of the equipment was in primary colors, the ground beneath padded with a layer of wood chips.

Drallmeier let Jackson run free and wild. Clouds blew across the sky, their shadows raced across the beaten down grass.

Clifton hadn't arrived yet.

He glanced at his Minnesota plates. It bothered him, but Drallmeier knew no one would really care. Residents of the two port cities swapped around easy enough, no one paid attention that oil and water never truly mixed.

Clifton had said, "My plates are from Michigan. Big deal." Drallmeier hoped he'd turned a corner.

He popped the trunk, pulled out Jackson's backpack, and set it on top of his car. Clifton said he wanted to take his kid to the U.P., the Upper Peninsula. Who was Drallmeier to say no? It did bother him that Clifton wanted the hand-off of the kid done on the sly.

"Don't mention it to Tina. Just throw some of Jackson's clothes together, toothbrush and what have you. It'll be a surprise, like a Mother's Day present for her."

"Mother's Day was over a month ago, man."

"Okay, so the present's late."

To meditate on Clifton made him so: he pulled up in his Suburban, a firetruck red vehicle pushing twenty years, rust detailing around the wheel wells. Drallmeier knew Clifton had nothing to speak of—Tina let him know—depending on temp jobs in the U.P., maybe his mother, maybe even less on his brothers and sisters, a catch-as-catch-can crowd up near Ishpeming.

Apparently the Suburban had no AC; the windows were all rolled down. Drallmeier bent to look in—four sweaty, rowdy kids. Clifton barked at them as he clambered out and they quieted. His canine demeanor didn't change for Drallmeier.

"Where's Jackson?"

The little boy was enjoying himself, boinging back and forth on a yellow frog attached to a tough spring with a lot of whang power. Clifton paid no attention to the racket.

"Where is he?"

"These yours too?" Drallmeier was joking.

"Yes. What of it?"

Drallmeier nodded at the children. They ignored him. How many women was Clifton involved with in the Twin Ports?

A neighborhood mom and her kids joined Jackson by the equipment.

"You taking them all to the U.P.?"

Clifton glanced around. "You son of a bitch. You didn't bring him, did you?"

Clutching the backpack, Drallmeier said, "I got as far as filling this, then I couldn't go any farther."

Clifton looked at the woman with the kids, then back at Drallmeier. "I should knock you on your ass."

Drallmeier waved at the kids. "Their moms know where they're going?"

Clifton strode back to the driver's side of the Suburban. "Fuck you." Exhaust fanned the street, the red vehicle with Michigan plates took the corner, likely on its way to Highway 2.

Drallmeier tapped the plate number into his phone. Jackson came running.

"Is my daddy coming?"

"Change of plans, man. When'd you last see him, anyway?"

Jackson shrugged, the concept foreign to him, as it would be for the rest of his life.

Blomfeldt's Paperboy

Blomfeldt, who would die in a Duluth hospice at the age of eighty-two, first had the dream in 1966 when he was still a detective with the Port Nicollet Police Department. The dream through the years skipped back like the needle in the groove at the end of a LP, the tone arm failing to automatically lift, the thup-thup sound, and he was back in the head of Patrick Severson, the fourteen-year-old paperboy. Over time he told himself it was his subconscious, that he was apparently too dense to follow it through to the end. "Chet, if you could just be Patrick's eyes and ears from four a.m. to six a.m. that Sunday morning, you could solve the case. You could give Mr. and Mrs. Severson an end to it."

But the thing was, when he was about to close in, the alarm would go off, or his first or second wife would wake him, or his four children clambered onto the bed, anything that would fit a poorly scripted crime drama turned it off. The face of the killer would vanish in the smoke from the 55-gallon burn barrel, the ignition a soft explosion.

He leaves the stuccoed two-story house at 16th and Marquette before sunrise. Mom had woken him, made the cocoa and toast before going back to bed. She left the radio on, a church program from Duluth, but he turned it off. There's just the sound of his dunking the toast, slurping it up, and sipping the hot chocolate. Before heading out to the garage for his wagon and wire cutters, he scoops a handful of his little brother's Cap'n Crunch from the box on the table and fills his mouth, a few square yellow bits fall to the table and floor. He forgets to turn off the kitchen light. The seconds tick by on the clock above the fridge.

Early Sunday morning is quiet in his neighborhood. There might be someone from a graveyard shift driving down North 21st Street and he hears a bad muffler with the light traffic further off on Beacon Avenue. His empty red wagon clanks between the square concrete slabs of the uneven sidewalk.

His plans for this summer afternoon are many: argue The Beach Boys versus The Beatles with his best friend Joey—Patrick likes The Beach Boys and plans on going to California someday—play a little baseball out behind Roosevelt, catch some of the Twins-Tigers doubleheader on the transistor radio up in his bedroom. Mom mentioned two options for dinner. The Sveden House Smorgasbord on Beacon. He loves the pink slabs of baked ham sharing a plate with a yellow mound of macaroni and cheese. Or a spicy pepperoni pizza and a Coke at Dominic's, eat it right at the shop under the mural of Port Nicollet's lakefront painted by a local artist. The artist taught at the high school and he would go there in a couple years.

Roosevelt Elementary is a block away and in little time Patrick is there, cutting diagonally across the blacktop behind the school, past the painted foursquare and hopscotch squares, past the basketball hoops, the doors to the gymnasium, aiming for the burn barrel, the stacks of newsprint there beside the barrel at the corner of North 22nd Street and Rusk Avenue. The tires of his wagon ring like an empty, rolling metal barrel.

It's Blomfeldt's nurse charting at the computer, checking the tubes connected to his body. She sings a song that he doesn't recognize. She likes her job. His second wife, Patti, tired with care, sits at his bedside and strokes his bristly cheek. He needs a shave and he loves her so much.

"Good morning, honey. Father Anthony is stopping by." And Blomfeldt's eyes closed, back to Port Nicollet, across the bay, east of Superior, in 1966, back into Patrick's head.

He could do it in his sleep, clip the wire from around the thick Sunday editions, stack them in the wagon and start out down North 22nd. Glancing around, he sees the car, red with white panels, the one he'd seen last weekend. It pulls up.

"Father," Patti said.

The car door opens and there is the darkness.

Patrick Severson was found dead a week before his fifteenth birthday in a field of tall, weedy grass on Speedway Avenue. It was 9:08 p.m., Sunday, June 26, 1966, seventeen hours after he left home. His wagon and wire cutters were missing.

"Father is here," Patti said, but Blomfeldt was already gone.

Acknowledgments

This book's existence is due in part to the encouragement of the editors of the publications where some of the stories first appeared in earlier forms. I thank them, gratefully acknowledging:

"Frenesí" in *Close to the Bone*

"Closing Time at Mom's", "Payday Friday", "The Forcier Brothers", "Playdate" in *Shotgun Honey*

"Taste Your Lips of Wine" in *Mystery Tribune*

"Sukiyaki" in *The J.J. Outré Review*

"Far from Home" in *Crime Factory*

"The Ballad of John Rider", "Boomer in the Sky with Toxics", "The Price of Copper and Brass" in *Tough*

"Deep Cuts at the Inner Groove", "Counterweight", "Suburban Creep", "As Good on Him as on a Dead Man" in *Yellow Mama*

"Like a Strange Old American Folk Song" in *Flash Fiction Italia*

"At the Head of the Lakes" in *Mysterical-E*

"Barman" in *Rock and a Hard Place Magazine*

"The Hardest Part" in *Wisconsin People & Ideas*

"The Ice Shoves" in *Pulp Modern Flash*

"The Effects of Urban Renewal on Mid-Century America", "Blomfeldt's Paperboy" in *Mondays are Murder*

"Mile Marker", "Uh-Oh, Love Comes to Town" in *Beat to a Pulp*

Also, to the writers, poets, and memoirists who make up the St. Croix Writers group. Thank you for giving me the opportunity to read many of these stories to you in their early versions, Tuesday mornings in Solon Springs, Wisconsin, and over the telephone during the pandemic.

To Zakariah Johnson, the talented short story writer and novelist, thank you for being the go-to reader and reviewer of this collection prior to my patting it on the head and sending it on its way. Thank you for all of that, as well as your honesty and friendship.

All due obeisance to Steve Fox for pointing me in the direction of Cornerstone Press. Thank you for giving me a clue, Steve. I'm happy I picked up on it.

To Cornerstone Press: Thank you, Dr. Ross Tangedal, Director and Publisher; Brett Hill, Editorial Director, and his editorial team; Chloe Verhelst, Production Director, and her team; and Carolyn Czerwinski, Production Editor, for the brilliant cover design for this book.

To my personal local historical society, my parents, Alvira and Adolph Esterholm, who gifted me with their recollections of the Twin Ports, Superior, Wisconsin, in particular, from the 1930s to the 1950s, everything from changes in public transportation and local businesses to the Tri-State Fair and the location of the Gitchinadji Town and Country Club. Thank you for sharing the long ago with me. The region is an anchor for my fiction. Also, thank you for letting me read whatever I wanted to read when I was a kid—so very important, considering today's world. Love to you both.

And to the one who has given me the time, the space, and the belief—at times, sorely needed, that belief—my love, my wife, Suzette. Thank you for the years.

JEFF ESTERHOLM is an award-winning story writer. His fiction has been published widely in *Midwestern Gothic, Shotgun Honey, Wisconsin People & Ideas, Beat to a Pulp, Crime Factory, Mystery Tribune, Pulp Modern, Tough, Yellow Mama*, and many other venues. He is a past winner of the Larry and Eleanor Sternig Award for Short Fiction from the Council for Wisconsin Writers. He lives in Superior, Wisconsin.

Printed in the USA
CPSIA information can be obtained
at www.ICGtesting.com
LVHW092243071023
760480LV00007B/58

9 781960 329080